NICOLA VICECONTI

Come With Me

Translated from the Italian by Laura Bennett

Aspal Prime

Published in Great Britain in 2021 by Aspal Prime,
an imprint of Aspal Press Limited
1 Quality Court, Chancery Lane, London WC2A 1HR

Originally published in Italian in 2017 as 'Vieni Via'

Copyright © Aspal Press Limited, 2021

All rights reserved. No part of this publication may be reproduced, stored in a retrieval system, or transmitted, in any form or by any means, without the prior permission in writing of the publisher or as expressly permitted by law.

This book has been translated thanks to a translation grant awarded by the Italian Ministry of Foreign Affairs and International Cooperation.

Questo libro è stato tradotto grazie a un contributo alla traduzione assegnato dal Ministero degli Affari Esteri e della Cooperazione Internazionale italiano.

A catalogue record for this book is available from
the British Library

ISBN 978-1-9162895-3-6

Printed in Great Britain by Book Printing UK, Peterborough

www.aspalpress.uk

The characters and events in this novel are fictional and as such do not correspond to real people or situations.

Contents

The Discovery	1
Strange Precautions	15
Paris-Moscow, a One-way Ticket	27
The 'Pioneers' of Via Tiburtina	37
The Accident	44
Intuitions	63
The Wings of Freedom	82
Igor Smirnov	94
Coyoacán	102
El Gordo	111
San Miguel de Allende	121
El Descanso	134
Juanita the Curandera	145
Going Home	162
And Now… the Present	172
Notes	178
About the Author	179

The State is my father. It gives me work, a home, a salary, takes care of my health, sends me on holiday, educates my children and when I die, it will bury me with dignity, at its own expense. [1]

The Discovery

Paris, 19th July 2015

They tricked us, Franco. They tricked us! They duped us with their ideology, their propaganda and their imaginary paradise of justice and liberty. They destroyed us. They wiped out our love, as if peoples' hearts were anything to do with them. You understood what they were like before I did. No soul and no conscience! That's what you said that time at the hospital. How could anyone be indifferent? The time to tell people has come. Please. You're someone who can, so do it for me too!

Just a handful of words before Irina vanished into the darkness. She was thin, very thin, if it hadn't been for her unmistakable eyes, I wouldn't even have recognised her. It was very painful seeing her again. Her cheeks were dirty with earth and she had a large grey bruise across her forehead, which was more furrowed than I remembered.

I woke up with a start and a muffled scream that came straight from my throat, as if I had regurgitated it. The scream rang around the room for a few moments, then silence fell again on that hot and suffocating night.

It was still dark. I sat up and stayed there, my forehead beaded with sweat and my face fixed, thinking and rethinking what I had been asked to do. It was the third nightmare to strike me in a matter of days and Irina's message was always the same. She wanted me to look back over episodes in my life and explain how I had managed to keep my reason, never sacrificing it on the altar of an ideology that had been instilled in me since childhood.

No small thing given that I would have to untangle the internal jumble of my spiritual, ethical and political conditions and leave behind a 'state of minority,' as Kant called it.

I must have explained this concept to my students dozens of times and I always started with the way regimes usually wield political power. 'Obey without reasoning' I would write on the blackboard, careful to note the reactions of the class. It was a provocation, I realised that, but it was very effective in stimulating an interesting debate that would last for hours and resume, sometimes even with brighter moments, over the days that followed.

In my case I had to ask myself how I had used reason when making two types of choices: those determined by circumstances that were imposed on me and those that came from being a free and thinking man. Now I can say that I succeeded, definitively.

To shake off my slumber, I got out of bed and went into the dining room. I picked up a bottle of cognac from the drinks trolley and drank a couple of sips. I felt the alcohol burn right down to my stomach, then took the Gauloise packet and lit one. I've been buying this brand of cigarettes for a lifetime, since I decided to come to Paris to live in 1963, or rather, when the city chose to adopt me.

I took a few greedy puffs before leaving the cigarette to burn out in the ashtray. A rivulet of thin bluish smoke snaked sinuously up towards the ceiling. I followed it with my eyes while I wondered how much the inevitable conditioning of chance or my will had affected my decisions. The eternal struggle between the inevitability of destiny and a person's determination...

Normally, I never think about death, but that night I felt a strange anguish, as if it was about to show up at any moment. It's not death that scares me, but the possibility of not being ready should I have to face it without warning, just as happened to Giovanni three months ago.

Giovanni Zampi was like a brother to me. As well as sharing the Paris apartment for the last fifty years, we shared a childhood, an adolescence and a long spell of political militancy. He was a great pianist and a member of the Paris National Opera. I have to recognise that he played a decisive role in convincing me to tie up the loose ends of the past. He had already dealt with it in his own way by writing a book in 1993 called *The Two Sides of the Coin*, recounting his misadventures across Europe. But I had barricaded myself for years behind absurd justifications that have turned out to be merely an awkward attempt to flee from my responsibilities to the truth.

I did try a few times, but whenever I did, I wasn't sure who I was talking to anymore. Who should I share my disappointments with? The party leaders? Impossible. Most had been dead for years and the few survivors, representatives of a protected species, had undergone a profound transformation just to tread water in the changed political landscape. Giovanni said intuitively of their attitude that this was just the beginning, that they had only lost the first layer of modesty and things would continue to get worse. So? Who was I supposed to talk to? My parents before they died?

That would have been no use, they would never have believed me. And besides, I had tried in the winter of 1963, when I went to them with proof. Not even then would they acknowledge the evidence.

That was why I kept going for a few years, deluding myself about the power of forgetting, which turned out to be a crude attempt to block the hatch to the past with the boulder of hypocrisy. I will die wondering how I managed to believe such a solution and make such a miserable mistake. As a human being, I can say that I have sinned naïvely, but as a professor of history and philosophy, I will never be able to forgive myself for the error I committed. In the name of forgetting, I even changed my identity and invented a new name: Enrico Ceccarelli instead of Franco Solfi. A story that only Giovanni knew about.

But forgetting is a boomerang that comes back around to strike you when you least expect it. Only an idiot could believe that pages can be removed from history because someone decrees it that way. It means denying memory and the course of events; a practice now so widespread as to conceal the truth from those affected by dictatorships. An expedient activated in the name of a so longed-for national reconciliation.

Yet if this path is taken, the risk of leaving wounds open becomes too great. I am reminded of an Argentine singer-songwriter who, in a song dedicated to memory, warns:

The Discovery

'memory awakes to wound those who don't let it live free like the wind'. In the end I realised that the solution in my case might not be having to forget at all costs. The only thing to do was to reconstruct the mosaic of part of the past piece by piece.

To do this, I had to embark on a long and tortuous journey when I least expected it. A path that took me first to the East, to a land where the cold and wind reign supreme, and then to the other side of the ocean. Now that I've come to the end of this experience, I can say I finally feel free and at peace, towards myself and others.

Giovanni was convinced until the very end of the need to tell people about what we had seen: 'People like us have to make their experiences available to historical truth. It's the least we can do to allow younger generations to understand how things played out in that part of the world!'

I never replied to his definition of truth which, in my opinion, was far too simplistic. It is clear that the events and facts produced by human beings determine the collective history of a people that, in this sense, the search for truth can only define as historical. But we must remember that in the kaleidoscope of a thousand truths, there is one that has been experienced, linked to the vicissitudes of particular individuals who have personally lived through specific events. A definition that I certainly did not invent myself and that refers not to the official story handed down to us from the system with the imposition of sinister propaganda, but to the one that comes from people as the sum of their personal experiences, states of mind, enthusiasm, frustrations and disappointments, told by flesh and blood men and women. Gathering these testimonies can help remove the veils that have covered some aspects of history for years. I believe this is the basis of *not forgetting*. And I also believe that there is no absolute truth in ideologies or doctrines because they are made of thought, and thought, at best, can point to the truth, but never *is* the truth, or the whole truth.

It was almost dawn when I fell asleep on the sofa, with the air conditioner on. At 8 o'clock exactly, the maid took care of waking me up.

'Faustine! What are you doing here?' I asked, surprised to find her on the doorstep.

'Buongiorno Professore. I've come to do that job…'

It took me a moment to realise what she was referring to. I had put our appointment out of my mind entirely.

'We have to sort out Giovanni's things, remember?' she added as she walked through the door with an ease and mastery of the place she had long since acquired.

Faustine was referring to the emptiness that Giovanni had left in the house and in my life; she could certainly not have imagined that the night's insomnia was to do with a nightmare about Irina. Not that I wasn't suffering because of my friend's recent death, but it seemed superfluous to explain the real reason.

Faustine finished the sentence with a smile. We talked for a few more minutes, then I realised it was getting late. If we wanted to get something done, I would have to hurry.

'I'll just be a moment,' I told her as I went to my room to get dressed.

'I'll make you a coffee. It'll do you good. An espresso, obviously,' she joked, alluding to the fact that I only drink Italian coffee.

The Discovery

'I accept your offer. Let's see what you're capable of,' I replied, playing along.

Faustine is a tiny, dark woman with glasses. She is forty-seven but has been working in this house since the age of eighteen. I am as fond of her as if she were a daughter, even though I don't know what it means to have one. She is a good woman and a tireless worker. Despite the confidence that has grown up between us over all these years and my many invitations for her to call me by my first name, Faustine does not cross the line and maintains an obsequious form of respect towards me that does not allow her simply to call me Enrico: to her I am 'Professore'.

She is very capable. Her only flaw is the mess she leaves the bookcase in every time she goes near it. I've tried several times to explain to her that books are sacred to me and that, as such, must be respected, even by her. I've accumulated a huge number of them over my lifetime and have carried them with me through every move, as indispensable nourishment for the soul and the mind that I've never wanted or known how to do without. My books have a history, even their arrangement on the shelves of my bookcase respects a rigorous criterion that cannot be altered. But as far as Faustine is concerned, a book is only a pile of sheets of paper stuck together, an object to be dusted like any other.

That morning she had come to help me face the most painful moment since Giovanni's funeral. I was the one who had asked her to carry out a specific task. Unlike the first few days after my friend's death, during which, in an attempt to reject reality, I behaved as if he were still alive, I suddenly decided to get rid of everything that reminded me of him. It was a good way to shake myself out of the paralysis into which I had sunk after his death and to try to look forward. I couldn't go on living in a house full of his belongings and I freed myself of them.

I started with the furniture. I posted an ad on a specialist website and, within twenty-four hours, a newlywed couple from Meudon came to pick it up in a lorry. Then, with the help of Faustine, I filled some cardboard boxes with his belongings and donated them to charity. I put everything in them: paintings, shoes, clothes, old political magazines, his entire collection of precious pipes and a hundred or so musical scores. All I kept to remind me of Giovanni was his piano and an old photograph of the two of us, not yet teenagers.

Knowing I could count on Faustine's help, I even decided to tidy up the cellar, a space I had almost forgotten. Whenever I set foot in there, it felt like visiting a museum. The first thing I noticed on the rusty shelving was my old portable Olivetti, the one I had used in the Seventies when I was teaching at a high school in Rome. It was the 'Lettera 32' and, of all the models, it represented the most technologically cutting-edge version, definitely the easiest to handle and with an ultramodern design. Its practicality made it the favourite typewriter of journalists and perhaps, for this very reason, contributed greatly to a kind of writing that was fashionable at that time.

I grabbed the case by the handle, put it down on a table and pulled out the typewriter. I stood looking at it for a few moments before pressing a key. The metal bar hit the roller and got stuck. I tried another, but the result was the same. The space bar didn't respond well either; despite trying several times, the mechanism was jammed. I told Faustine to put it to one side, that I would take it to an expert to have it repaired, if I ever found one still capable of doing so and, who knows, maybe use it again from time to time or if I needed to.

We continued exploring among the dusty objects. In one corner, hidden by empty bottles and other junk, was a strangely shaped suitcase.

'Give me a hand, please,' I said to Faustine, as I tried to work out what it was.

'Is it yours?' she asked.

'No. Almost everything in here belonged to Giovanni.'

I took the suitcase and unzipped the sides. Then I opened it with a hint of fear, as if I was defiling someone else's property.

'What kind of instrument is it?' Faustine asked.

'It's a bandoneon,' I replied, carefully pulling it out of its case.

'Strange name. Is it a small accordion?' she remarked.

'Sort of,' I replied, 'the Germans invented it, but then it became famous in Argentina. Giovanni always said it was the instrument of tango.'

'Did he know how to play it?'

'I wouldn't rule it out. He enjoyed playing almost any instrument. He would say that, with a little imagination, they're all the same. This bandoneon was a gift he had been given by someone special. Here, read this.'

I showed Faustine a dedication engraved on a small plaque glued to the instrument case. On it was written: *'Per il maestro Zampi. H.B.'*

'Do you know who the initials belong to?' I asked her and added, pre-empting the inevitable shake of her head, 'to Heinrich Band, the man who invented it. Giovanni had got to know him in Germany'.

I don't know why I started explaining all the details about the bandoneon to Faustine, but I was pleased to see that she was interested.

It took us the whole afternoon to empty the cellar and, in the end, I felt satisfied. I was ready to leave when I realised that Faustine was still fiddling with something behind the door.

'What about this? What should we do with this?' she asked, inviting me to take a look inside a plastic bag she was holding open by the handles.

I approached intrigued.

'How did that end up here?' I asked, widening my eyes in amazement.

What an idiot I was to ask her such a question! What could Faustine possibly know about that old coat? I was very young when I used to wear it and she didn't know me then. The memories automatically brought me back to distant situations and I took myself off for a few minutes.

'Professore, are you feeling OK?'

'Yes, Faustine. Everything's OK.'

'So, it's your coat then?' I nodded.

'The last time I wore it was fifty years ago. I was sure I'd lost it,' I said.

'And now you've found it, what do you intend to do with it? It's in bad shape,' she commented.

'Nothing. I don't intend to do anything with it,' I replied impassively.

Faustine sensed a certain coolness in my few words and her tone became serious once more.

'Do you want me to take it to the dry cleaners?'

'No, Faustine. I'll take care of it. Don't worry.'

I was a little annoyed by her insistence. It was a moment I didn't want to share.

I grabbed the coat with both hands and brought it up to my face. Then I closed my eyes and took a deep breath.

'Professore, what are you doing? Can't you see it's covered in dust?' she exclaimed instinctively.

I stayed like that for I don't know how long, intoxicated by memories. To me that dusty fabric, with its unmistakably stale smell, hardened by time, was not simply a coat. It was the raw material to ignite my memories, causing them to burst into flame, a way of recovering fragments of a distant past, immersing me in the amniotic fluid of memory, from which I came back vibrant with emotions.

'It doesn't matter if it's covered in dust, Faustine,' I said. 'It doesn't matter.'

I sniffed the coat again as she looked on, astonished. Then, finally, we left the cellar and went back to the apartment. The bulk of the work had been done. Faustine changed, gathered her things and left. I put the coat, still in its bag, on the chair in the hallway and went out onto the terrace. Under the rosy light of a sunset sky, I gazed into space, over the rooftops of Paris.

Perhaps Faustine had taken offence at my tone, but I wasn't unduly worried. I couldn't interrupt my emotions at that moment: for me it was like being in a time machine. There is a relationship between our senses and the brain that can enhance the memory in certain situations and I chose to let myself be carried away, to a place where not even dreams can reach. I had established a connection between that smell and something that had remained buried in the maze of my mind and I wanted to hold on to that now somewhat remote sensation of the past to savour it slowly. The same thing had happened a century earlier to someone much more important than me as he described how he felt on tasting a tea-soaked *madeleine*. As had happened to Proust, with the taste of a simple cake, everything seemed clearer to me too: what I was looking for was not in the coat, but inside me.

...

The following day, as always, the alarm clock went off at a quarter past six. Once, at that time, I would have been getting ready to go to the university, but since my retirement from teaching, I have got into the habit of walking along the Seine. It's a new habit, a cultural and sentimental experience with this city that I have come to love. I go out when most people are still asleep. I like to be one of the first to welcome Paris as it reawakens. My route is always the same: I set off from the Quai Saint Michel, follow the river to the Quai de Montebello, where I stop to admire the Cathedral of Notre-Dame in the distance, before turning back, along the Rue Saint-Jacques. I finish my walk at the Saint Germain des Prés intersection, about a hundred metres from home. There is a news kiosk there, where I buy a newspaper which I then read sitting comfortably at a table in my favourite bar: Le Bistrot de l'Absinthe.

It is a place that has gone down in the history of Paris as one of the oldest literary bistros in the city. The tables now occupied by tourists who eat on the go were once the meeting places of painters, intellectuals, musicians and political refugees. They would discuss the world and life, developing theories and fashions that initially intrigued, then seduced intellectuals from other countries. Paris at that time was the engine room of the great ship of European culture and it was in places such as these that the most evocative works came to light and took shape.

The elderly owner had himself written theatrical texts of note and, in the Fifties, was part of the existentialist group, the intellectuals who focused on the experience and analysis of the disturbances of the human soul in the face of existence. Evidence of his commitment is demonstrated by photographs in which he poses smiling alongside Sartre and other members of his entourage.

Truthfully, there are also other reasons that bind me to Le Bistrot de l'Absinthe. The first is the wonderful bookshelf that can be browsed inside, an indispensable invitation to lose oneself along the paths of literature; the second is linked to absinthe. It is still possible to sample in this bar an excellent quality glass of the 'green fairy,' distilled in accordance with the long-standing French tradition. Absinthe has left its mark on history here. Suffice it to say that the bistro's first small sign, dated 1884 and kept as a relic in a glass case at the entrance, depicts a couple sipping absinthe. It was at this time that the drink was at its most popular in France and, as claimed by the American poet Ernest Dawson, doctors were even prescribing a glass a day. *'Absinthe has the power of the magicians; it can wipe out or renew the past, and annul or foretell the future'*, or so it was believed.

I don't know if the miraculous powers attributed to absinthe are true, but what you can undoubtedly sample in the bistro is its delicious flavour, entirely different from whiskey or beer which, also according to the American poet, are the drinks of fools.

As always, I let the taste of absinthe come out on my palate for a few moments before lighting a cigarette. Then I turned to reading: in addition to the newspaper, I had brought a story by Flaubert that plunged me into the world of the imagination. At eleven on the dot, I decided to leave, said goodbye to the old owner and left.

When I got home and caught sight of the coat again, I dived back into my memories. It was then that I decided to put it on, slowly, fastening the buttons one by one. Then, in an automatic gesture, I pulled up the collar and put my hands in the pockets. This was how I braved the cold when I was twenty-five, I thought.

I was curious to see myself dressed like that and went to stand in front of the mirror. It felt strange to notice the effects of the years on my body. Aside from the wrinkled face and completely grey hair and beard, the thing that struck me most was the image of a tired man who could no longer bear the weight of that old, now unfashionable, coat.

I was still there, intent on staring at my image, when I realised there was something in the right pocket. I checked it properly and spotted a small plastic bag attached to the lining with a tiny hairpin. I opened it and inside was a piece of paper with a short message. It was written in Russian and I immediately recognised the handwriting unmistakably as that of Irina.

I read aloud.

'Они прибывают. Чтобы получить меня и повезут в Vladivostok, приезжай забрать меня'.[2]

Strange Precautions

Someone had taken Irina to Vladivostok, away from me forever. What if that was really what had happened, I wondered in a low voice.

Even just the very thought of this theory sent a shiver down my spine. I dropped the coat on the floor and, still clutching the note in my hand, sank into the chair. I closed my eyes and fell back into the seat. I began to wonder about what had happened to her. While my eyes followed the words from one side of the piece of paper to the other, I heard their sound, as if she was saying them. Suddenly everything I had imagined about her vanished, bursting like a bubble.

Irina had disappeared from my life forever and in those long years it was all I could do to survive the emptiness she had left behind. After a long time searching for her in vain, I had even come to believe that she was dead. It was a peculiar mechanism of the unconscious to try to come to terms with it.

That message radically changed the situation, however, nurturing a thin thread of hope inside me that she was still alive somewhere.

'Irina, my love!' I shouted.

The walls of the room returned the echo of a strange silence. Suddenly, every noise seemed muffled: the tick of the pendulum clock, the music of my neighbour's radio, even the roar of the traffic from the street below seemed dulled.

The revelation before my eyes referred to a fifty-year-old situation that there was no doubt could not still have any bearing on reality. How could I have brought it back into my life now? Every time I finished re-reading the note, the meaning of those words vanished like a fleeting image in front of the mirror. However hard I tried, I couldn't keep the idea fixed in my mind of Irina isolated in a remote town in the far east of Russia. It seemed impossible to me that in a borderland I might be able to find the answers to the many – too many and all unresolved – questions I had always asked myself about her fate.

At the same time, however, the chance discovery of that note was so surreal that it represented a discontinuity in my apparent tranquillity. Irina had come out of nowhere to beg me for help, just as she had in my dream. She had done it by sending a message with a serious tone and dramatic content with which she had told me where they were taking her.

I slid into a whirlwind of conflicting emotions. At first, just having something of hers in my hands gave me a feeling of joy. Suddenly I felt the love that fate had made impossible and the inexorability of time had almost completely suffocated explode again inside me. Irina had come back into my life with the same disruptive force of the wind that slams shutters at the window before a storm, and with a presence that I felt more real than her own body. She had reached out to me to be heard and to reawaken in me a long-held desire: to look for her. 'Come and get me,' the message ended.

Immediately afterwards, however, I let myself be

overcome by feelings of guilt for not having found the note sooner. Who knows how things might have gone if I had read her request for help right away? I lingered over imagining a different path that our lives might have taken and a kind of remorse began to haunt me like a woodworm gnawing endlessly through seasoned timber.

Then the absurdity of that thought immediately brought me back to reality. How could I have noticed it if I hadn't worn the coat since that day? I dug inside myself to find the indispensable dose of rationality needed to answer the many questions that had been accumulating in my head in the meantime.

I spent the afternoon re-reading the message, hoping to grasp some information that went beyond the unequivocal literal meaning of those few words. It was then that I noticed Irina's coarse and imprecise handwriting. Her pen stroke was hasty and a couple of words were even incomplete. I knew her writing perfectly and had no doubt that she would never have written like that in a normal situation. Perhaps she was scared or knew she was being followed by someone and didn't want to be discovered.

A sudden memory emerged clearly, confirming this last theory. There were, in fact, two men just a few metres away from Irina the last time I had seen her. I had to put things in order in my head and reassemble every gesture to try to understand if I had missed something else. I lit a cigarette and concentrated on the memory of that afternoon. It was 12th November 1963, a Tuesday.

I was sitting in a chair and looking out through the windowpanes of a room in Moscow's Sklifosovsky Hospital. I was waiting for Irina so that I could tell her about the decision I had made to go back to Italy for a while. Despite objections from my parents, who had repeatedly reiterated what they thought about my convalescence, I was sure I would be treated better in an Italian hospital. Mine had become a complicated case in all respects and I had the impression that no one, except Irina, had understood the gravity of the situation.

This was my main reason for returning home. The suggestion of allowing myself to be treated in Italy was given to me by a young doctor who occasionally came to visit me. Unlike the others, I had a more spontaneous relationship with him, in the sense that when he talked to me, I didn't feel as if I was being controlled. I was myself, as was he. I remember he asked me for help translating some articles in an Italian scientific journal and I agreed. To tell the truth, there was also another reason behind my decision to leave: the atmosphere with my university friends had soured and there was no doubt that some distance from them and the party for a while would do me good. Knowing me, a couple of months would be more than enough to for me to get my strength back. I would return to Irina in great shape, intent on putting an important plan into action: marrying her. After all, getting married was our greatest wish, as well as the only way to try to build a life outside the Soviet Union. During my absence, Irina would have plenty of time to tell her parents, who had always been opposed to our relationship. That was also something I wanted to talk to her about on that Tuesday afternoon.

I had been in hospital for about two months recovering from a delicate operation on my leg and right shoulder. 'You're lucky. It was a bad accident,' the nurse told me as she took me back to my room after four hours in the operating theatre.

My room was on the first floor and directly overlooked the visitors' entrance hall. That afternoon at exactly five o'clock, visiting hours, Irina walked down the driveway that led to the surgery ward where I was recovering. I saw her go through the gate; she was wearing a dark overcoat and a red scarf the same colour as the hat that, only partially, covered her long hair. She was walking briskly with her eyes down, carrying her bag hanging from her right shoulder and holding a book in one hand. Once she reached the window, only then did she raise her head and our eyes met. I was happy to see her again after an inexplicable absence of a week and I greeted her with a smile, but she didn't flinch and continued walking up to the door. I wondered why she was being so cold; she was usually much more expansive. It didn't take much to make me suspicious: at that moment it was as if Irina had wanted to tell me something, but couldn't. 'What's happening?' I murmured, as I struggled to get up from my chair to greet her. A few minutes, the time it would take to climb a flight of stairs, and I would ask her about her behaviour. It was then that I looked back in the direction of the hospital entrance and noticed the presence of the two strange men I had glimpsed when Irina arrived. With a lightning-fast gesture, the pair passed something from one to the other before separating: the first, taller and heavier-set, took up a position near the door, pretending to read a newspaper; the other, skinny with dark glasses and a hat, walked quickly towards the exit only to get into a car parked on the opposite side of the road.

...

In recalling all those memories, I had rekindled the hope that Irina was still alive and that she was waiting for me somewhere. And even though, in all probability, she was no longer in Vladivostok, one of the most isolated cities in Russia at that time, that was where I felt I had to go. I swallowed hard to lighten a lump in my throat that had come for me at the very thought of seeing her again. Then I put my hands to my face and struggled to remember other details from my time in the hospital.

Day and night, I was guarded by nurses who had been categorically ordered by the hospital director not to leave me alone for as much as a moment. They had decided to adopt specific safety precautions for me, starting with the choice of room, which was rather isolated from others in the ward, and going so far as to perform rigorous checks on the very few people who came to visit me.

The surgery had been successful and I had been back on my feet for a few days. I had even very carefully taken my first steps again. Despite this, I wasn't satisfied with the rehabilitation programme they had put me through and was anxiously waiting to be discharged from the hospital, although this was slow in coming. Nobody could tell me for sure when they would discharge me. I spent those days in a surreal atmosphere of monotony – suspicious of everyone around me – and silence. I was living at the mercy of a conjecture that soon proved to be fatal for the love story between Irina and me.

I felt confused, lacking the energy to claim my rights. I asked to be able to get in touch with the only contact I had at the embassy, but it was futile. The only phone call they allowed me to make was to my parents, but they didn't believe my version, nor did they listen to my request to return to Italy.

As far as they were concerned, I was just exaggerating:

'I've already explained to you, Franco, the Sklifosovsky Hospital is one of the most renowned in the world. You're in excellent hands. There's no point your returning to Italy,' my mother had said before ending the conversation. It was as if everyone had joined forces to keep me under control. It was this that led to my almost instinctive decision to want to leave.

I would have liked to talk about my intentions with Giovanni, but I never managed to see him. A month after being admitted to hospital, I found out that they had prevented him from visiting me. The nurse on duty told me one evening: 'Your friend Giovanni has asked for you several times, but the security people have always denied him permission.' I didn't hear anything more about him for some time after that.

Not even Irina could tell me what was happening. Despite being the daughter of a colonel, she too was subjected to rigorous security checks every time she came to visit me.

Today, after reconstructing the whole story in the smallest detail, I can say that those days spent in hospital were the hardest of my life. They extended my hospitalisation orders from above. I was in a sort of stand-by in which everyone who interacted with me played an exactly preordained role. The task of the doctors in the days that followed my operation was to provoke a sense of confusion in me by occasionally giving me Pentothal. I found out by chance, when the nurse absentmindedly left my medical records on my bed. It was a very popular practice among KGB agents at that time, an effective way of digging into people's minds to get to their secrets or simply, as in my case, to make them forget certain episodes.

Try as I might, I couldn't remember anything about the accident. Officially, I was responsible for a violent rear-end collision on the E101 state road towards Moscow at Aprelevka. To corroborate this theory, they even showed me a local police report that spoke of the involvement of a second car, whose driver, the only person who could testify to what had really happened, had died instantly. For years I believed this version, the only one that was given to me. Then I discovered that the truth was quite different.

There was also another reason behind the continuous administration of barbiturates: to verify that I was unaware of any information concerning the activities of Irina's father.

...

Irina must have been on the stairs when the two men entered the room, picked me up all of a sudden and took me straight down to the basement garage in a service lift. They covered me with a blanket and made me get into an ambulance: 'I'm Ostap Galkin. We're moving you to another facility for security reasons,' said one of the two men.

'For security reasons.' I repeated the words in amazement while they were taking me who knows where, as if I were a package. Something about my relationship with Irina was getting complicated, but I couldn't begin to imagine why. From the way they moved, it was clear that the two men were intelligence agents.

I knew their methods well and didn't resist, as it would have served no purpose. The ambulance left the hospital with its sirens off and we found ourselves in the heart of the city. It was snowing continuously, the flakes coming down heavily and silently. Why this sudden transfer? Where were they taking me? And above all, why was someone deciding my fate?

We were heading towards the airport when, almost there, we turned right into an isolated area. We arrived in front of a barracks that I obviously didn't know existed. Once inside, destiny mocked me even more.

I spent two days in the infirmary of that barracks, during which I tried in every way possible to get an explanation. Every time I asked something, I got the same reply: 'Security reasons,' the agent on duty would repeat. They were all so secretive that I couldn't understand what was happening to me. Once again, I was forbidden from using the telephone. When I asked insistently to speak to Comrade Sorgi, the party representative at the university, they replied that it had already been taken care of. I didn't sleep at night, pretending to myself that everything was fine; it was all a misunderstanding and that nothing would happen to me. After all, I had nothing to fear and sooner or later someone would come to explain the reason for these precautions.

Despite everything, I began to dwell on my behaviour. What if they were angry with me for going too far in my classes? I was reminded of the final reprimand my university tutor had given me on observations I had made about Marxist ethics. 'Positions disconnected from the ideological principles of socialism,' he told me in a reproachful tone. Or that time they had summoned me to the police station to order me not to divulge works by Russian authors published clandestinely as *Samizdat*.[3]

The next morning, they brought me some clothes and ordered me to get ready because I was about to be discharged from the infirmary. At nine o'clock a police officer showed up accompanied by an official from the Ministry of the Interior who gave me a piece of paper: it was documentation of my expulsion from the country. I read it without batting an eyelid, as if I were not its intended recipient.

Giovanni had foreseen that moment a couple of months earlier, when I had told him about the meeting at the Hotel National with Irina's father. 'You're pushing too hard,' he said. 'Sooner or later, they'll kick you out of the country.' I answered with a shrug and he was annoyed by my flippancy. '... And know that if they do, you should consider yourself lucky.'

I was well aware of what Giovanni was referring to when he talked about luck in certain circles and for certain situations. Back then, the unlucky ones were interned in some psychiatric hospital, disappeared in the basement of the grey palaces of power or in places so remote as to not appear on any map. It was impossible to trace them. Despite this, I was unable to hear or fully understand his words. I was enchanted by Irina and, like everyone who falls in love, I was living imprudently.

The expulsion order with immediate effect had been formalised on my residence visa by the minister's initials: 'Expulsion of the Italian citizen Franco Solfi from the Soviet Union'. In the middle of the document was a Russian red ink stamp: 'EXPELLED'. My gaze fell on the reasons for the measure. I had been branded an 'unwanted person': a generic way of classifying the country's ideological enemies.

Strange things happened in my mind. Although I had in my hands the confirmation of my immediate removal from Moscow, and therefore from Irina, the first thing I thought about was finding her. I couldn't know that at that same moment, she too had been the recipient of special provisions, nor could I know that they had already sent her to Vladivostok. I didn't have the coat with me; they sent it on to me in Italy two months later, with the other belongings left behind at the hospital.

'I want to speak to Irina, Irina Shestakova,' I said, folding the deportation document and putting it back in the envelope.

'I'm sorry, Mr Solfi, we have specific instructions,' replied the ministry official.

'I need to see her!' I replied, raising my voice.

'I've already told you: we have specific instructions. In two hours, you will be on a flight to Rome and will leave our country.'

'Then I want to speak to Colonel Shestakov'.

There was a silent pause during which the pair exchanged a glance. Then the police officer left the room and I remained alone with the official. It was he who clarified definitively what would happen over the hours that were about to follow.

'It isn't in your interest to make a fuss, Mr Solfi. You have no alternative. And as for Shestakov, you would do well to forget the name. This is a warning.'

He also left but I was on my own only for a few minutes.

I felt fear, but not for my physical safety; if they wanted to hurt me, or seriously scare me, they could have already done so. The feeling of fear was linked to the future. I had been in Russia for four years and never felt like that before.

Unbeknown to me, I was a victim of the same plan enacted against Irina that involved her removal to Vladivostok at the same time as my immediate expulsion from the country.

This was how Soviet activism was: drastic and effective interventions capable of solving underlying problems. And as far as some Soviets were concerned, I was a problem.

The police officer came back to tell me that a car with the engine running was waiting to take us to the airport. I could only think of Irina with those men on her heels. Surely, once she found my room empty, she would have realised they were splitting us up. That must have been when she decided to put the note in the coat pocket.

Paris-Moscow,
a One-way Ticket

'Some emotions are too intense to be allowed to fade. They must be experienced if you want to avoid having regrets.' This was the first thing that crossed my mind the moment I read Irina's message. I sat motionless, pursuing a voice hammering like a stuck record, always stopping on the same word: 'go'.

About twenty minutes must have passed, an eternity for my troubled and confused state of mind. I moved the various theories around in my head like pawns on a chessboard, without ever finishing the game. Suddenly, however, like a skilled chess player, everything seemed clearer to me and I chose the right move.

What strange tricks the mind plays when we make certain decisions! There is a part of the brain that is activated automatically, in which thoughts are structured unconsciously and transformed into concrete actions without 'ifs' or 'buts'. This is the psychological function in which emotions prevail over the rational control of reason. These bodily sensations can influence the mind and even spring out of individual details, such as the emotional nuances we absorb during a simple conversation, the sounds and background noises we hear during the day, the sensations we feel when we touch an object or, as in the case of the old coat, memories that are still alive, triggered by a smell. Once we cross over into the emotional realm, it's not long before we start acting spontaneously and this is precisely when we free ourselves from mindless conditioning.

And so, a week later – the time it took to obtain a visa from the Russian Embassy – I found myself on a train to Moscow. Attracted like a cobra by the sound of music, I went on a journey of discovery, inside and outside myself, looking for the courage to face life again.

It was clear that the purpose of this trip was to see Irina again, but at the same time, it gave me an experience that finally made me feel alive. After the forced separation and desperate attempts to find her in the first few months after my expulsion from the Soviet Union, Irina's absence had pushed me to live in a limited world in which, apart from Giovanni and a few others, I saw practically no one. It was as if I was living inside an enclosure, moving around in the same space and always talking to the same people. This was the price I had to pay for transforming myself into a new person: a fugitive sheltered and isolated from everything and everyone, who wanted to bury his past.

I don't even know how to describe my loneliness. Perhaps as a halfway house between something forced on me by what had happened and something I had sought out voluntarily. What was certain was that it was not an ascetic practice that involved me looking inward for ways to improve myself as a person. Nor the means of reaching 'true wisdom,' as Schopenhauer might have put it. I believe that the loneliness into which I had been sucked for years, and which I always considered a means rather than an end, was of the kind that comes about despite the presence of others. I sacrificed the spontaneity of a relationship with those close to me and had to keep a safe distance, like porcupines do when they huddle together to keep warm but end up pricking each other.

Irina's message offered a different reality from the one I had created and she made me realise I had made a serious mistake. With the decision to leave, I did justice to Irina once and for all, to our love story, calming the turbulence of my soul caused by a kind of repentance for the choice, albeit forced, I had made.

I decided to travel by train for two reasons: on the one hand, I wanted to enjoy the landscape of a Europe I had almost forgotten; on the other, I needed to give myself the time needed to reflect on some episodes of my life spent with Irina. A thirty-six-hour journey seemed enough to take stock of the situation before I suddenly found myself catapulted into the past.

I have always loved travelling by train. I must have inherited the passion for it from my uncle Renato, my father's brother, who spent fifty years of his life as a train driver. After roaming Italy from north to south, he took up a post as a driver on the line that went from Rome to the lake at Castel Gandolfo. It was the Fifties and, to the delight of Romans, this, one of the most scenic routes in Central Italy, had recently been opened. On Sundays, people would cram into the train from Termini Station to enjoy a trip out of the city; when he could, Uncle Renato would take me with him so I could look down on the beautiful lake below. I remember him holding me tight as I leant my head out of the window; the air of the moving train was so strong

Come With Me

that I couldn't keep my eyes open. It was an extraordinary feeling and when I opened my eyes, it was as if the trees were moving around me, not the train.

Once Uncle Renato let me into the cab, sat me on a stool in front of the control panel, pointed to a lever and said: 'Go on! Pull it!' I must have been ten years old and everything seemed huge to me. I sat still on that stool with my head down and legs dangling, feeling my heart pounding in my chest with excitement. Then I mustered the courage, slowly looked up beyond the glass and glimpsed an expanse of vineyards stretching up to the foot of the hill. 'Pull it before the tunnel!' my uncle repeated with a firm voice. Only then did I grab the lever with both hands, close my eyes, take a breath and pull hard. The train whistle echoed around the valley, causing birds perched on telegraph wires to take flight. We entered the tunnel at high speed, while my uncle and his colleague laughed with satisfaction. I felt proud of what I had managed to do and couldn't wait for the chance to tell my friends at school. I was still holding onto the lever with both hands when the train came out of the hill and we found ourselves facing the lake that reflected the warm sun of the Castelli Romani.

When I called Faustine to tell her I was leaving, she was speechless: the sudden decision to go on a trip seemed inconceivable to her.

'Are you telling me you're leaving for Moscow tomorrow?' she asked, surprised.

'Yes, Faustine. I can't put it off any longer.'

'And what are you going to do up there?'

'I need to go back to some places from my past.'

'Why Moscow? Isn't Rome your city?'

Faustine's observation was correct. Then again, she knew I was of Italian origin but was completely unaware of the time I had spent living in the Soviet Union, including my relationship with Irina.

'I'm leaving for Moscow,' I replied, without providing any further explanation. 'I'll let you know when I'm coming back.'

'OK, Professore,' she added after a long pause. 'I will take care of the house.'

I sensed a veil of unspoken disagreement and poorly concealed apprehension in her tone of voice.

'You don't have to worry about me, Faustine. I'm still capable of looking after myself,' I replied, playing things down.

'That's not it, Professore. It's just that…'

'Don't worry. It's a personal thing and maybe I'll tell you about it one day'.

I didn't keep the conversation going and said a hasty goodbye.

Faustine could understand my state of mind simply by the tone of my voice – she knew me so well – and she had sensed that I was about to do something unusual. She understood the reasons for my reserve and had the foresight not to ask me anything else. Finding Irina in Russia after fifty years was like looking for a needle in a haystack, I knew it, but I had made up my mind and I wouldn't have backed out for any reason.

I got to the station early. The taxi driver unloaded the only bag I had and motioned for a porter to accompany me. The train was already at the platform as the passengers were beginning to look for their seats. I had reserved the sleeping carriage for the night and a seat in the passenger carriage during the day. I had chosen one by the window so I could enjoy the landscape. The first stop on the route would be Strasbourg, followed by further stops in Germany's main cities before entering Russia through the new republics of Eastern Europe. Arrival in Moscow was scheduled for around midnight the following day.

I stowed my suitcase and sat down. Meanwhile, a recorded voice informed passengers about arrival times at the various stations. Sitting on the seat opposite was a young man in an elegant suit and fashionable glasses; he greeted me with deference, which I returned with a nod. He was talking on his phone about capital and investments; I only had to listen to the conversation for a few minutes to understand that he was a Parisian entrepreneur, one of the many who, with the worsening of the crisis in the country and across Central Europe, had diverted his capital to the East. He was talking about an agricultural machinery plant in the province of Minsk, in that part of the old continent now called Belarus, but which in my day was still part of the Soviet Union and known as White Russia.

Sitting next to me was a rather showy lady in her fifties, intent on leafing through a magazine. She turned the pages at a frantic pace, without stopping to read the articles and glanced at her phone, which she had placed in her line of sight on the armrest of her seat, with compulsive frequency. I later found out that she was Russian and was returning to Moscow after spending a week's holiday in Paris. The obsessive ritual of the magazine and phone stopped a few moments later, coinciding with the train's departing whistle. Only then did the long convoy begin to move and, in no time at all, we were leaving Paris to enter the verdant countryside of Champagne-Ardenne.

I was excited, perhaps even a little frightened by the uncertainty of the situation I was getting into. After all, I didn't know exactly where to go, let alone where to turn. I was motivated only by the power of hope. From that moment, I felt the need to isolate myself from my travelling companions. I was returning to Moscow, once the homeland of communism, the place that had inexorably marked the destiny and experiences of so many men and women who believed in the ideology and had given their lives to one of the most important collective political undertakings in modern history.

A remote corner of a picturesque Europe, the city of Moscow has always provoked conflicting feelings of love and hate in me. While I remember the moments I experienced with Irina fondly, I will also never be able to forget the political disappointment that began maturing in me during my first spell at the university.

Irina and I were in our early twenties when we began collecting the most intense emotions of our love story: from wild rides along the banks of the imperial Moskva to passionate kisses in front of Saint Basil's Cathedral; from a giant snowman we made with friends in Red Square to afternoons spent in the Bosco Café, inside the historic GUM department store; from walking past the Kremlin Arsenal, arm in arm in the dark, accompanied by the icy stars of a firmament that winked at us knowingly, to the scent of our bodies lost in a passion that was never sated, an emotional zeal that found no peace and continually renewed our joy of living and loving each other.

I closed my eyes for a moment and even thought I could taste the birch sap that Vladimir, the elderly comrade who worked in the café, would make for us.

To be exact, the first time I set foot in Moscow had been a couple of years earlier. I was nineteen and had already been in politics for some time. It was 1957 and the party had organised a trip to the Communist World Youth Festival. Also in attendance, I remember, was Pier Paolo Pasolini, correspondent at the time for the weekly *Vie Nuove* magazine published by the PCI. The event involved delegates from different countries, debates, official speeches by representatives of the PCUS and guided tours of the capital's symbolic sites.

I travelled by train that time as well. Twenty of us set out from Rome, all registered at sections in the Tiburtino and Nomentano districts. In the workers' homeland we found ourselves full of enthusiasm, eager to breathe the air of revolution and tackle debate on the fundamental issues of the Marxist dialectic.

Despite the general euphoria, however, even under those circumstances I was already getting the impression that there was something about the Soviet model that did not convince me. Genuine room for discussion between the agreed delegations and party representatives was reduced to a minimum; the contents of the programme had been set out from above and not from below, as we would usually organise our Feste dell'Unità events. The festival was reduced to a procession by the official regime in accordance with a protocol so tight that it failed to grant any freedom of movement to the participants. During our time in Moscow, we were channelled and forced almost exclusively into official meetings with no room for unscheduled visits.

But of course, a single impression is never enough when it comes to understanding such complex dynamics. The context and short timeframe of that first visit to the Soviet Union did not allow me to realise something that I was instead able to see much more clearly in 1979 when I returned to Moscow to attend university.

I had passed the selection organised by the party to identify students and activists deserving of going to Russia. The decision to go down that route had the full consent of my parents, both communists. My mother and father believed the experience at Moscow University to be a fundamental step in the training of a true communist. Even my mother said that what I was about to make was an important life choice that not everyone had the opportunity or good fortune to achieve. I was a communist too. At that time, I was like all the members of my family: my father, my uncle Renato, my mother, her sister Beatrice and so on, all the way to my second cousins. I grew up in the euphoria of militancy within the Communist Party without asking myself too many questions or considering the nature of my affiliation.

Yet, the first time I took part in the selection, I was unsuccessful. Despite presenting myself with good credentials, for political activism while at secondary school in particular, I had failed to prepare enough to convince the party official in charge of the selection. The interview to assess the depth of my knowledge of party history went badly and that first failed attempt was a real setback for my parents. My mother refused to speak to me for three days; she found my hesitancy in explaining some of the facts relating to the Salerno Turning Point hard to swallow. I tried again the following year together with Giovanni. The same official was in charge of the assessment; he was a tough Stalinist. I still remember his name: Edoardo D'Onofrio, a key figure in the party and the politics of the Roman Communist Federation.

Unlike the first time, I didn't even give him time to finish asking the questions: like a river in full flow, I began recounting the history of the party. When at the end of the interview, staring me in the eyes, he asked: 'Why do you want to go to Moscow to continue your studies?' I got up, pointed to Russia on the map behind him and replied: 'To feel how the wind whistles in that part of the world.'

The 'Pioneers' of Via Tiburtina

We had been travelling for four hours and were nearing Strasbourg, the first stop on our journey across Europe. In the meantime, the young entrepreneur and heavily made-up woman had struck up a conversation that was surreal to say the least: while he talked about spreads and finance, she enthusiastically shared details of her Parisian shopping experience at the Louis Vuitton atelier. They tried to involve me on a couple of occasions, but I was careful not to accept the invitation. I found their subject matter tremendously boring and I also had other things to think about: I wanted to remember how my interest in politics had first come about and which episodes had left the greatest mark on my past as a young communist. To do this, I had to go back through the phases of my life as far as the dawning of my adolescence, when I was about ten years old.

Being politically active at such a young age might seem strange, but in my family it was normal. In those days, interest in public life was widespread among all sections of the population. They were the immediate post-war years and, as was the case with my parents, many were keen to commit for the good of the country.

Those who supported the Americans and the Marshall Plan concerned themselves with politics. Then there were the representatives of the new right, who were the hardcore supporters of the fascist experiment. Politics was also of interest to those who simply wanted to continue protecting their own interests, those who were constantly looking for support so as not to waste the wealth they had accumulated during the war. Finally, there were the workers, who swelled the ranks of the left-wing parties: the socialists on one side and the communists on the other. Every member of my family belonged to the last group, with conviction. For them, after years of dictatorship, being political meant carrying out a mission that had as its main objective the defence of the freedom recovered through partisan struggles.

Of my relatives, Uncle Renato was the most battle-hardened. He was famous in the railway workers' union for his sensational action plans. He would always say that the railway workers were the most feared of all the workers because they could paralyse the entire country with a strike. There was no doubt that this was true; I realised it once when they blocked the trains passing through Rome's stations for a week.

Back then, there was a continuous coming and going of people in the Party section. The neighbourhood secondary school students had volunteered to distribute pamphlets. My father, armed with a brush and paint, as well as lime and a bucket, had made banners to hang from the railway bridges at Tiburtina station, the closest to our home, where the striking workers had organised an impressive command post. My mother and other female party members took care of the food and drink to be handed out to the demonstrators, while we kids went back and forth between the section and the occupied station forecourt. We had been given the job because we could run like the wind and knew all the shortcuts to avoid the carabinieri trucks.

Giovanni and I would race to see who would get there first. We would fly along the Via Torlonia as far as Piazza Bologna, then, after crossing Via Stamira, run on down to the union headquarters. There, on a stage marked out by red flags, Uncle Renato and other comrades would hold improvised rallies to tell the citizens about the reasons behind and aims of their mobilisation. The demonstrators would shout their protests with chants and slogans praising Lenin and Stalin. The myth of communism hovered overwhelmingly in that atmosphere and I was there, breathing the air deep into my lungs.

Sometimes, we would take the shorter, quicker route via the railway, arriving at the command post from below, walking along the tracks. We were barely teenagers and it all seemed like a game; only later did we understand that by carrying out these tasks for the party, like every young militant, we were performing a real rite of initiation, with a bravado typical of our age.

Giovanni and I wanted to make a good impression on the strikers and were always willing to lend a hand, if not two. Some of them gave us sweets, others reciprocated with a pat on the back; for us, these simple gestures were more than enough to make us feel part of the group, part of the action. In the evenings, after intense days of rallies and debates, the strikers would transform their stronghold into a party, where comrades from different districts would gather around large tables. Giovanni and I would play impromptu football matches and hold tug-of-war competitions with other kids, under the amused gaze of our parents.

Sacrifice, excitement and fun: for me that was the world of communism and, in no time at all, I allowed myself to be infected and captivated.

It is fair to say then that I forged my political identity in a natural and spontaneous way. I let myself be seduced by an ideology, adherence to which, for the members of my family, was taken for granted, considered almost natural, and irrevocable.

There were many kids like me scattered across Rome and we brought vitality and joy to the party sections. The older comrades called us 'pioneers,' and Giovanni and I were just some of those from Tiburtino, the most numerous. We were the children of a period of suffering, born to parents who had been punished by the fury of fascism and war. It was their life stories that determined our ideological belonging, through a visceral imprinting, not acquired through book learning, but decidedly more erudite and intellectual.

Initially, it was my mother who left an indelible impression on me and led me to take a political side. I have to admit that her attitude towards communism was consistent and irreproachable to the last. 'Remember that the truth can't escape,' she repeated on her deathbed when, in her local Piave dialect, she took stock of her life. The roots of her ideological adherence to the party lay in the death of her brother, mowed down by a machine gun on the Karst Plateau during the Great War.

The paradox is that I too have always supported my position by appealing to the same concepts of justice and truth. When I saw my mother for the last time, I had already distanced myself from the communist ideology. She was dying and I had neither the strength nor the will to insist on making her understand my point.

The same feeling of pain and helplessness in the face of mourning for loved ones had also been felt by father when, after the first Allied bombing of 19th July 1943, he found himself digging in the rubble to extract the bodies of his mother and sister. He was barely twenty when, with the help of firefighters, he laid their battered bodies down on the dusty tarmac. Others, desperate like him, silently gathered pieces of families blown apart by the bombs. Early that morning, my father had gone with his mother and sister to the home of an aunt who lived in Piazza Pontida in San Lorenzo, the neighbourhood worst hit by the 'carpet-bombing' inflicted by the Americans on the Italian capital.

The memory of the sound of the sirens in the distance announcing the tragedy, my father's desperate race from one side of the city to the other in the hope of saving them, the feeling of suffocating heat, the acrid and pungent smell of explosives mixed with the dust of houses razed to the ground, the sky made to feel artificial like a flickering plastic cloak are just some of the memories of that terrible day that he carried with him for a lifetime.

My parents' communist and at the same time anti-American position was passed down to me through the idea of an open confrontation with the party that had changed the most, in no time at all, into the symbol of American interference in Italy: the Christian Democracy.

In the face of these adversaries, we 'pioneers' played a very specific role: that of 'troublemakers'. We attended their rallies and demonstrations in large numbers to make a din or distribute PCI leaflets provocatively.

Our commitment increased during the 1948 election campaign, when the Christian Democrats, in order to persuade Italians not to vote for the Communist Party, organised the so-called 'Exhibitions of the Other Side'. These collections of anti-communist political propaganda were aimed at portraying the Bolsheviks as ruthless and dangerous. Communists were depicted as barbarians, violent and, above all, cruel beings who ate children. This was the tone of the exhibition. 'Mothers! Save your children from Bolshevism!' read one poster that showed a child cowering under the hammer and sickle. The youngster had a terrified expression on his face as he begged for help with outstretched arms.

No sooner had the posters gone up on walls around Rome than we would intervene. Sometimes we would even go as far as Piazza del Gesù to remove those that had been stuck up in front of the main Christian Democrat headquarters. Giovanni and I would go there at dusk; he would station himself in front of the door to check that no one was coming, while I would tear them down one by one. Then we would run away, screaming at the top of our lungs '*Viva Stalin! Viva Togliatti! Viva il Partito comunista!!*' The first few times my legs trembled with fear, but the more we did it and the more success we had, the easier it became.

Those expeditions were like a game for me, in which I enthusiastically took part. They were real political actions, however, and, as such, involved an element of risk. In retrospect, despite my young age, I should have thought about what I was doing and taken a little more time to consider my feelings towards the situation that had swallowed me up completely like quicksand. I had become part of the escalation of hatred between two political factions that could perhaps have competed with each other in a different way. As would happen to me in Moscow ten years later, I could also have developed a greater awareness of what I was experiencing back then.

Today, I can say that only when you remain independent from political doctrines can you think for yourself without succumbing to that endemic conformism that drags in and involves anyone who, blinded by ideology, takes sides impulsively. There was no shortage of facts to provide food for thought during those years: Tito's split from Stalin, the rise to power of the communists in Czechoslovakia and the Hungarian Revolution were just some examples.

It should also be admitted that the spiral of political violence was caused mainly by the obtuse attitude of the party in power at the time. I'm referring to the asphyxiating repression with which the Christian Democrats always addressed the communists. A repression to which the most battle-hardened comrades, such as the former partisans, reacted harshly. While we young 'pioneers' limited ourselves to tearing down posters, distributing copies of *Rassegna Sovietica* magazine or, at most, disrupting rallies, they began to radicalise the conflict to the point of civil war.

I had first-hand experience of the consequences of this type of attitude at the age of fourteen when, after being a 'pioneer,' I was thrown out of secondary school in my first year for my behaviour, for active participation, with other pupils, in a student cell of the FGCI.

The Accident

27th July – 00.35 am

The train pulled into Moscow's Belorussky station a few minutes late. I felt a strange excitement as I stepped onto the platform. Finding myself back in Russia was like suddenly reliving something that belonged to me. The abrupt transition from the still air of the sleeper carriage to the crisp air outside woke me from the numbness caused by the endless journey. I sighed and walked towards the exit. Once outside, a busy and noisy city overwhelmed me; it was completely different from how I remembered it. For a moment, I wasn't even sure I was in Moscow. But that feeling didn't last long; all it took was for me to read the sign for Zastava Square and I was brought back to reality.

I walked a few steps forward and stopped to look at the stalls of a market set up on the station forecourt. Despite the late hour, the square was packed with people attracted by street vendors intent on displaying products of all kinds. There were all sorts of things: clothing, household items, mobile phone accessories, books, antiques and various knick-knacks. You could even buy Red Army memorabilia, such as soldiers' uniforms and deactivated rifles that had been used against the Germans in the Second World War.

Among the visitors there was even the odd Russian citizen, always ready to regret times gone by, the irreducible communist, the dyed-in-the-wool Leninist-Stalinist. I recognised him from the way he paused to read a copy of *Pravda* that a stall-holder kept displayed on a lectern like a sacred text. I went over to browse and read the title of a five-column article dated 20 April 1937: 'The tasks of the proletariat in the current revolution'. Despite having distanced myself from communism for years, I felt a great interest in what I was looking at; it was the first publication of the summary of the April Theses that Lenin had declared a few days earlier, on his return from Switzerland, a document of great historical importance.

I realised this was only the first stage on a sort of Via Crucis that had been laid out for those most nostalgic for the former Soviet empire. Moving forward slowly as if in a procession, I found myself in the midst of a group of people who had gathered to hear the words of another of the main leaders of the October Revolution: Joseph Stalin. It was the famous speech that the Bolshevik revolutionary had delivered before the Soviet people at dawn on 7th November 1941 to incite resistance to the Nazi-fascist advance that was preparing to invade the country. People listened to the speech in religious silence and finally expressed their satisfaction with prolonged applause. Alongside me, an elderly couple were poised with handkerchiefs in hand ready to wipe away the tears of emotion; behind me, a man waved his clenched fist at the sky, cursing America and Europe.

The more I entered into that reality, the more I became aware that the Russia I had left behind had been transformed into a complex country in which present and past coexisted in a tangible way. Getting lost among those stalls was like immersing myself in a story full of contrasts, an inevitable step in being able to acknowledge the incessant change in the Russian people, starting from the fateful date of the fall of the Berlin Wall.

The air was heavy with a mixture of smells from a nearby rotisserie. A scrolling red LED display advertised the dish of the day: *pasta all'amatriciana*. I wondered if that was another of the effects of Western contamination.

I continued wandering around the multicoloured bric-a-brac. A trunk full of memorabilia contained the photographs of every president of the former Soviet Union; these were displayed alongside those of rock stars who had performed in recent years at the Olympiyskiy. A huge poster of Pink Floyd captioned 'Live in Moscow 1989' showed David Gilmour in the foreground, smiling, in front of the Kremlin. Not far away, another group of people had gathered around a large screen to watch a video of the uproarious anti-Putin protest staged by Pussy Riot in the Orthodox Church of Christ the Saviour. At the stall opposite some tourists were listening to a Russian guide talk about the history of Moscow from the post-war period to the present day. The young woman pointed to a poster showing one of the regime's many parades, that of 1st May 1956, organised on the occasion of workers' day. I listened to what she was saying for a while, then shrugged my shoulders and walked away disinterested. I found the tour guide's attempt to gloss over the repressive aspects of the Soviet regime in favour of showing a cleaner side of socialism at any cost decidedly mystifying.

I couldn't stand these kinds of reconstructions. I had personally experienced the social injustice, backwardness and neglect of the Soviet Union in the early Sixties. What kind of an impression would I have gleaned from a speech so steeped in ideology?

What a strange paradox ideology is, I thought: an intrinsic attitude of the human spirit capable of determining a particular understanding of the world, yet when it is defended it can lead to wars and genocides. How perverse is its connection to human passion!

I still have vivid memories of how excited I was the first time I set foot in the famous Red Square. At that time, Marxist thought held a fascination for many Italians like me, who had been seduced by the socialist model. It was the time of a dream of a new society, a political and social example that we comrades of the PCI had learned directly from activism and which could not be found in any European capital apart from Moscow. Like so many back then, I too believed in ideology and I did so by subjugating myself to the suggestion that exploded inside me after listening to speeches by communists who would never question the party line, nor ask questions about their own actions. I realised this especially when I was living in this city to attend university.

Despite everything, I understood the guide's attitude. On the other hand, as Levi argued, the more radical the revolutions, the more they tend to preserve the traces of the good that existed in the past. The young woman's message was clear and aimed at safeguarding Russia's romantic past, lived before the wall came down, a sort of pro-Russian attitude that the recent Ukrainian conflict had even managed to rekindle. An interpretation of history that glorified the image of Russia as a 'country of egalitarianism' in which, even if the party leaders did enjoy some privileges, there were neither rich nor poor, just as there was neither inflation nor unemployment. Her biased presentation was also aimed at safeguarding the image of Russia described at other times in its history, referring to love stories and the heroic deeds of great men and women.

The other Russia, that of the Gulag and purges, was too distant a memory to recall, because it belonged to very few survivors.

I looked at my watch and saw that it was after 1 am. I decided to spend the night in one of the many hotels near the station. I crossed the square, still sniffing at everything I came across like a bloodhound. The city I knew no longer existed and the one I had found had been given a makeover and embraced Europe.

The first thing that caught my eye was the heavy traffic and the many foreign cars. And to think that when I lived in Moscow, the few cars on the road were almost all Soviet-made! The short walk to the hotel was more than enough to give me further and clearer confirmation that everything was different, that, as well as imported products and the newness they brought with them, even the people had changed.

I spent a few more minutes focusing on the details my first image of Moscow had given me. Then, tired but satisfied, I went into the Hotel Pushkin and enquired about a room for the night.

Despite the tiredness and late hour, it took me a while to fall asleep due to a sudden thought that began buzzing obsessively in my head: the truth about the accident. For years I had harboured doubts about what had actually happened, my suspicions growing with each passing day.

The next morning, I was supposed to leave for Vladivostok to look for Irina, but I decided to change my plans slightly. I had with me the accident report they had given me in hospital and I could use it to trace the name of the commissioner in charge of the police station in the town just outside Moscow at the time. He would surely be able to tell me something about how the events had actually unfolded.

Aprelevka wasn't that far away and I thought about hiring a car.

28th July

All I had to do to track down Dimitri Golubev, the commissioner who signed the accident report, was ask a couple of local people. The first person who gave me information was an elderly woman selling flowers in the square in front of the former Moll factory, once the Soviet Union's largest vinyl disc-producing plant.

'Ah! Dimitri?' she said with a pitying tone, 'Who in town doesn't know him? You'll find him at the kiosk in front of the hospital. That's where he spends his days now he's on his own.' Without me asking, she also provided further details about the current situation of the person I was looking for.

Confirmation of the former commissioner's troubled life was given to me by a young man on a bicycle whom I had asked for directions. He was the one who accompanied me to the kiosk and pointed out the man sitting on a bench nearby. I sat in the car for a few minutes watching him: he was alone, with a cigarette butt dangling from the corner of his mouth and a bottle of vodka in his hand. Rather thin, he had bony shoulders and a hollow face. He was wearing a noticeably creased dark jacket and a wide-brimmed hat. He wore an expression of suffering and a sad gaze, looking who knows where. The word about town was that he had been on the receiving end of a real shock that had made him misanthropic and frustrated since his wife had left him to move in with a young engineer from Saint Petersburg. Others claimed he had been reduced to his current state by his terrible vice of betting on the horses. As well as his house and life savings, he had lost his wife and was living in poverty. Other rumours about him attributed the cause of his depression to the disappointment he had suffered in his professional life. Having believed in the system for forty years, in the early 1990s Golubev had publicly denounced a network of corruption that was rife among his colleagues. For the interview given to a Moscow newspaper he was fired on the spot; just a few years shy of retirement, he found himself alone, thrown away like a pair of old shoes.

I instinctively felt sorry for him and, for a moment, thought about leaving him in peace. It didn't seem right to bother him about a story he may not even remember. But then, moved by the desire to know the truth about what happened to me, I got out of the car, crossed the street and walked over to him.

'Are you Mr Golubev? Dimitri Golubev?' I asked in a firm voice.

He looked up slowly, took half a puff of smoke without even removing the butt from his lips, grimaced and stared back at the bottle of vodka. It was as if he was paralysed, but I took that sneer as a positive response.

'Someone who remembers me...' he muttered under his breath.

'Not exactly. I've never seen you before!' I replied.

'So, what do you want? A drink?' he answered sarcastically, offering me the bottle.

I looked at the amount of vodka in the bottle to try to work out how much he had drunk. Although it must have been about half, he didn't seem drunk. I refused the offer with a wave of my hand and brought the subject of the conversation back to the reason for my visit.

'Look at me carefully!' I continued. 'Do I remind you of anyone?'

'That's a difficult question, sir. I lost my memory a long time ago and I really don't think I can help you,' he answered, swallowing another sip.

'Many years have passed, but if I tell you my name, I have no doubt you'll remember,' I went on.

'I can assure you, I've forgotten the names as well as the people,' he replied dryly. 'Leave me alone!'

Golubev was closed off and bad-tempered to start with, evading any attempt at a conversation. I carried on for a few minutes, trying to make him understand how important it was for me to find out information about something that had happened in Aprelevka many years earlier. I told him he was the right person to reconstruct the facts, but he kept looking at me without saying a word. After several unsuccessful attempts, I gave up hope of his cooperating and decided to leave. I felt as if I had drawn a blank and wasted precious time.

'To hell with Dimitri Golubev!' I said to myself. I had made the trip to Russia to look for Irina and not to waste time with a decrepit, retired and perhaps already alcoholic commissioner. Without saying any more, I turned my back and walked towards the car. It was then that Golubev's attitude changed.

'Wait!' he exclaimed. I turned around.

'Don't waste any more of my time, please,' I replied, annoyed.

'Tell me your name then.'

After so many years, I was about to introduce myself with my true identity. It was the first time. The feeling was the same as when you see the light at the end of a tunnel and you get closer and closer to the exit. You rush, you gasp for air, but the fear of the unknown always remains because you never know what lies beyond the darkness. I took a breath and said my real name in a loud voice and with some embarrassment, as if I was referring to someone else.

'What did you say?' asked Golubev, jerking his head up.

'Franco Solfi!' I repeated, walking a couple of steps closer.

On hearing the name, the former commissioner opened his eyes wide and let himself slip into a moment of silence. Then he put the bottle down on the bench, got up slowly and raised both hands to his face.

'Solfi... the Italian!' he shouted in surprise.

'In flesh and blood,' I replied, holding out my hand.

He returned the gesture automatically, never taking his eyes off me.

'How did you end up here?' he asked incredulously.

'It wasn't that difficult,' I replied, showing him the report with his signature that I had taken out of my jacket pocket.

Golubev reached out and grabbed it, glancing at it quickly before remarking: 'I thought you'd died that night.'

'Died? But how? You signed the report, didn't you? Here, look,' I said, pointing to the section of the document where he had described the accident in minute detail. 'It's a description of a rear-end collision on the E101 state road, remember?'

'Of course I remember. How could I forget?'

'So, why are you confused? It was the other guy who died, the one travelling in the car in front of mine. His name is here too, look.'

Golubev threw the cigarette butt on the ground, rolled his eyes and sighed.

'There's no need to get so fired up. I filed that report and I know exactly what happened that night.'

'So?'

'The truth is different, Mr Solfi. I'll tell you everything.'

We went into the park. It was then that Golubev noticed my slight limp. He pretended as if it was nothing, even though he had clearly understood it was a result of the accident, a posthumous one I've been carrying around with me for a lifetime and which I've found it impossible to learn to live with.

'That's how it is, Golubev. Fifty years is nothing and there are some things you take to your grave,' I said to relieve him of his awkwardness.

'I'm sorry!' he answered.

'Forget it. Do you have any idea why I came here?' I asked.

'I think so. I must be the only witness to the accident, the only one you could trace, I mean.'

'Exactly, and now I've found you, I'd like to know the truth.'

Although I felt a sense of relief at the former commissioner's apparent willingness to talk, I felt a strange foreboding about having my suspicions confirmed.

'Yours is a terrible story, Mr Solfi.'

'Please can you reconstruct what happened step-by-step?'

The ex-commissioner took a photograph of a woman out of his wallet and showed it to me.

'It was our wedding anniversary and we were celebrating. In the middle of the evening, I received a phone call and had to interrupt dinner to rush to the police station. I left my wife still sitting at the table while I wondered what was so urgent. When I got to the office, I found two Secret Service agents who began giving me information about you.'

'What kind of information?'

'They showed me a file about you, basically the result of seven months of tailing you. Your movements in Moscow, the places you went to, the Russians and Italians you were friends with, your contacts at the university and the party were all listed in detail. The file also contained information about a friend of yours, a musician if I remember correctly, and about Irina Shestakova, the daughter of an influential and respected colonel.'

'Did they tell you about Vladivostok too?' I asked instinctively.

'Vladivostok? Definitely not,' he replied with surprise. 'What's Vladivostok got to do with it?'

I'd asked him the point-blank question to try to ascertain if he was aware of Irina having been taken to Vladivostok. If so, I would have the confirmation that both kidnappings had most likely come about for the same reason. But Golubev was completely in the dark; Irina and I represented two separate cases.

'What else did they tell you?'

'The meeting with the KGB agents lasted about half an hour, the time it took to receive instructions about an operation that had been classified as top secret.'

'What operation?' I asked.

The retired police officer sighed. He then admitted what the goal of the two agents had been: 'To take you out!' he said, slowing his pace. I suddenly felt a shiver down my spine, buttoned up my jacket and pulled up my collar.

'They had orders to kill you!' he repeated.

Golubev continued the story by describing in detail the first phase of the sinister plot hatched against me and shedding new light on what, at the time, was dismissed as an insignificant car accident. The naturalness with which he recounted the episode was disarming, but I couldn't help but listen to every single word. I felt a feeling of anguish sensing the weight of the bureaucracy of the Secret Service again, especially when I realised that the description of the two agents fitted those who had taken me from the Moscow hospital when a decision had come down from above to kick me out of the Soviet Union.

'What were the instructions?' I asked.

'Just to patrol the state road from 10pm. Those were my orders'.

'Are you telling me that was all they asked you to do? That was it?'

'More or less!'

'You got to the scene of the accident quickly then?'

'Yes. They told me the exact kilometre by radio.'

'Why didn't you ask the two agents for more information?'

Golubev laughed, instinctively but bitterly.

'I didn't need to know anything else,' he observed. 'You amaze me with your naiveté, Solfi! You must've forgotten how things used to work in this country: KGB orders could neither be refused nor discussed!'

We started talking about the accident again. I wanted more details about the collision.

'Do you remember anything about that night?' he got in before me.

I tried to re-explore the part of my brain clouded by the Pentothal, but my thoughts came back to me with a thud, like steel marbles against a rubber wall.

'The only thing I remember is that I was on my way back to Moscow after spending a day in Naro-Fominsk where I'd gone to meet a university friend.'

Golubev took me by the arm: 'Try harder, Solfi. You really don't remember anything else about that evening?' he repeated the question.

'I've already told you, it's like I have a hole in my memory.'

'Were you travelling alone?'

'Yes.'

'You don't remember a roadblock?'

His insistence took me by surprise. A police commissioner should have been perfectly familiar with the methods used by the KGB to wipe portions of memory from people's minds. I interpreted that question as confirmation that he was completely extraneous to the entire operation, at least from a certain point on, from the hospital stay where I had been subjected to the administration of barbiturates.

'No!' I replied.

'But you were detained for at least an hour at a police station after being stopped at a checkpoint near Druzhba.'

Once again, I concentrated on chasing after thoughts now lost in a labyrinth, no longer able to distinguish real memories from the images conjured up by Golubev. Suddenly the scene of a police car on the side of the road and a policeman ordering me to pull over emerged from my clouded mind. It wasn't a clear memory, but a series of fragments of scattered images that I struggled to piece back together.

'Wait a second!' I exclaimed. 'Yes, I think I do remember something like that.'

'I told the officers to stop you,' added the ex-commissioner.

'Did they detain me with a proper excuse?'

'Yes, I told them to follow you for a routine check.'

'Then what?'

'One of them drove your car.'

'A fat policeman! Now I remember. There was a fat policeman at the checkpoint.'

'It was Sergeant Popov. He was there that night as well.'

'Where did they take me?'

'I told you, to an old command post we had abandoned to move to a new location.'

As Golubev reconstructed the story, other images resurfaced from the recesses of my memory. Without realising, we had walked all the way around the park and found ourselves sitting on the same bench again.

'Was it inside a school, a library or something like that? I remember a green gate,' I said.

'Yes. Exactly, the former command post was next to a school and you had to walk down a tree-lined path to get there.'

'Were you there too?'

'Yes. I spied on you from behind a door. That was when I saw you for the first time.'

'What did you think in that moment? Did you know they were going to kill me? Or not?'

Golubev didn't answer.

'You might as well confess now, so many years have passed!'

'We weren't allowed to think…' he said.

'You've already told me that! You worked by following

orders from above to guarantee the serenity and stability of the regime. I'm well aware of how it worked, but is it possible you had no hesitation in cooperating in an attempt to kill someone?'

Suddenly the former commissioner's face darkened.

'I've never killed anyone!' he answered firmly, 'and I won't allow you to make insinuations like that.'

'But the system you worked for did though,' I replied in the same tone.

'That was how the world worked back then! As for your case, let me remind you that if the two agents allowed me to browse your file, it was only to show me that you had been marked out as a dangerous subject. The rest was none of my business. The order to intervene came directly from the Lubyanka offices. What else do you want to know?'

'Nothing, forget it,' I concluded by asking myself why, when it came down to it, I insisted so much on wanting to know his opinion on the plan the Secret Services had hatched and implemented to eliminate me.

'Of course I was shaken up!' he exploded. 'Some decisions were hard to accept, especially when it came to younger people like you, but what could I do?' That night when I got home, I even talked to my wife about it, violating the absolute secrecy I had been ordered to abide by.'

'Don't worry, Golubev,' I answered, reflecting on the fact that too often the boundary between the powerlessness of our actions and the justification of certain behaviours that ensue is so thin that it's easy to make mistakes. And Golubev had made a mistake: instead of saying what he thought, he had chosen to lie down and obey. The same difference that existed between my behaviour and that of my classmates at the university.

'I found out they were going to kill you just after that,' he continued with his justifications, 'and even if it hadn't been me that carried out the attack, do you think it was easy for me to always follow orders? The KGB had chosen the Aprelevka police station to support the operation. That's how they got to me and it wouldn't even have been the first case on the E101 state road. Other people like you had already been hit, all Westerners who had come here dreaming of communism.'

'Doesn't that strike you as a paradox?'

'Yes, perhaps. But, as I said, we were right at the height of the Cold War and that was the climate at that time. Soviet counterintelligence saw enemies everywhere.'

'And when they didn't find them, they created them,' I interrupted.

Golubev took off his hat, ran a hand through his hair, then placed it back on his head and stood up giving me the impression he wanted to bring our conversation to an end.

'You've said it well: counterintelligence knew how to create enemies. They were everywhere and this generated an obsessive attitude both in those who were in charge of the country's security and towards those under suspicion. In those days, even a simple conversation like this would have been the subject of an immediate KGB intervention.'

Golubev was right that I had not been the first nor would I have been the last in those years to attract the attention of the Secret Services: not infrequently, the gap between the ideals of communism and the harsh reality of the regime caused disappointment and dissent in European idealists. In which case, the system reacted, leaving behind it a trail, often forcibly ignored but always bloody, of victims, and I was supposed to be one of them. Giovanni had also been marked out by the KGB and, as he confessed to me many years later, was saved thanks to a concert he gave in Vienna. He had a premonition about not going back to Moscow, accidentally evading a plan designed to get rid of him. People like me and Giovanni Zampi were thorns in the side of the Soviet Union's reputation at that time. Our curiosity to thoroughly understand the system was considered nothing but a provocation and our spontaneous criticisms were classified as intrusions of bourgeois thought to be radically wiped out.

I pushed the image of Giovanni out of my mind and came back to the present.

'Please carry on. Where were we?' I asked.

Golubev's face was impassive. Perhaps he was angry at my provocations.

'There was an auto workshop at the back of the building. That was where they took your car while they kept you in the office on the pretext of a bureaucratic technicality with your residency permit.'

'Why did they take my car to the garage?' I asked.

I hadn't even finished asking the question when I found the answer written in the ex-commissioner's eyes. It was then that I was certain that the things I'd been watching in films for years had become reality, and to my detriment from that night on.

'They sabotaged the car...' I said in a low voice.

'Yes! With a tool to wear the tyres so they would explode at high speed,' he answered.

'So, it wasn't an accident?' I asked.

'It was an accident, yes, but as the result of tampering with the right front tyre,' Golubev replied. 'By the time they let you go I was already at the spot where they were expecting it to explode.'

'Go on.'

'I'd been given orders to stop the traffic in both directions to make it easier, but something went wrong.'

'What do you mean?'

'A lorry suddenly turned onto the road from a country lane. You tried to overtake it to miss it and at that moment the tyre exploded. Your car swerved and crashed on the opposite side of the road.'

'And where were you?'

'In my car, hidden behind a tree, ready to intervene. I was with Sergeant Popov. We saw the vehicle moving slowly and your car speeding past as you overtook it. Then, in the distance, we heard the crash of crumpling metal sheets. By the time we got there, the farmers driving the agricultural vehicle you'd overtaken were working, struggling in the light of their only functioning headlamp, to carefully extract you from the wreckage of the crashed car. You were in bad shape and they laid you out on the ground. They were pretty shaken but stayed nearby, not imagining that their presence was unplanned and that two witnesses greatly complicated the artificial picture of the situation.'

'Why does the report mention a car that I was supposed to have collided with and a dead man?'

'You didn't die at the scene as expected and there were two eyewitnesses. The KGB agents gave the orders by radio to call an ambulance and have you taken immediately to the Moscow hospital, where they would take care of fixing things.'

'What happened to the witnesses?' I asked.

'Sergeant Popov took their statements and sent them away. We gave them a different version of the report from the one they gave you in hospital. I heard nothing more about Solfi, "the Italian", after that.'

Golubev got up slowly. His eyes betrayed his anxiety and haste to leave. 'Solfi,' he said again in a dull voice, 'I hope I've been useful to you.' Then he adjusted his hat and left saying a peremptory goodbye and without a second thought, nor did he turn back for a final melancholy glance.

There were still many unresolved questions about what had happened after the accident: my stay in hospital, Irina's last visit and the reasons for my expulsion from the country were only some of them. However, the meeting with Golubev had given me some of the important pieces I needed to recover the truth about the attempt on my life.

Their plan to kill me in Aprelevka had failed and, thanks to a series of circumstances, the KGB agents were forced to give up on the idea of finishing the job in hospital. As Golubev had imagined, it would have been child's play for them to kill me, but clearly my close links to important members of the PCI, known at the top of the Kremlin, led them to find another solution. The long period of hospitalisation gave them the chance to develop the idea of distancing me immediately from the Soviet Union.

Intuitions

29th July

I decided to fly from Moscow to Vladivostok. It was the only way to cover a distance of about five and a half thousand miles – three times the distance I had travelled by train from Paris – in just over eight hours. I spent most of the flight looking out of the window, losing myself in the immensity of Siberia. I was at an altitude of thirty thousand feet and time seemed to be suspended in limbo, like the clouds that spread out like a compact carpet beneath me. My thoughts about Irina had suddenly built up so much that they wouldn't give me any peace, nailing my mind to a single question: where would I start looking for her? It was the awareness that I was getting closer and closer to the place to which she had been forcibly transferred that agitated me. This was confirmed when the pilot announced our descent towards Vladivostok airport. What was I supposed to do once we landed? Who could I contact for information about her? I had embarked on the journey in the hope of finding a trace of Irina, a simple clue that would lead me back to her, but how? I certainly couldn't wander around the city, asking passers-by if anyone knew her or had ever heard her name.

Nor could I contact the registration office, an idea I had already investigated before leaving Moscow. The name Irina Shestakova did not appear anywhere, not even in the telephone directory.

On leaving the airport, I took a taxi to the centre; the driver dropped me off at the entrance to one of the many bars on the famous Ulitsa Admirala Fokina. Instinctively, I glanced inside and saw that it was packed. Many of its drinkers had oriental features or were young soldiers on leave, singing Russian songs in an accent I could barely understand. They were probably sailors from the Pacific Fleet, the Russian naval fleet that had been based in the port area forever.

Vladivostok, like all maritime cities, was a melting pot for different peoples and cultures. In the same way as I had experienced on arriving in Moscow, change was once again in the air. It was no longer the small border town I had imagined; instead, I found myself confronted by one of the largest urban ports in eastern Russia, an outpost of the Chinese border, a place that had been designated a closed city in the late Fifties, accessible only to Soviet citizens with a special permit to live there. From the first time I saw it, the city seemed huge, greatly complicating my attempts at investigation.

Imagining that I would have to stay for a few days, I decided to get a hotel room. The owner was a man of Armenian origin in his fifties, who immediately took a liking to me for the mere fact that I was Italian. It was lunchtime; I chatted with him, then left my suitcase in my room before going out again. I spent all afternoon walking, scouring every corner of the city centre. During the days that followed, I extended my search to the port area: like a tireless detective, I decided to sift through all the cafés, restaurants, supermarkets and anywhere I might meet women of a certain age, but there was no sign of Irina. Once I even thought I had seen her inside a church, but when I approached for a closer look, I realised it had just been my imagination playing tricks on me.

Seven days passed and the idea, brought about by my disappointment, of returning to Paris became more and more pressing. In that short period, I had experienced first-hand the impossibility of taking on such a difficult challenge, something only someone stubborn like me could have attempted. The city was too big and I had no clue which area to target. Given those conditions, it would have taken a miracle for me to meet her.

The intuition about who I needed to contact to get news about Irina came to me unexpectedly on 5th August when I was talking to the hotel owner. I had made up my mind that morning to go to the first travel agency I saw to buy a return ticket to Moscow, when a remark made by the hotel owner made me think about something I had yet to consider. The Armenian had guessed the reason for my visit to Vladivostok, coming to that conclusion by way of a conviction: 'You see, sir, my father always used to say that no one ever winds up here by chance,' he said.

'Really? That's an interesting theory,' I replied intrigued. 'What reasons do you think would cause someone to come here?'

'Well, it depends on when you're talking about. Look,' he said, showing me *Les nuits de Vladivostok*, which he was reading, propped up on the desk. 'In this novel, set in the present day, Vladivostok is a hotbed of crime.'

'Could that be the reason then?'

'No, it was just an example. I was just trying to say that, unlike how things used to be, the underworld reigns here now.'

The Armenian went on to list a number of problems in modern-day Russia, emphasising social inequalities, the scourge of drugs and rampant corruption. It seemed as if he was telling me the entire plot of the novel by Christian Garcin, which he was still clutching in his hands.

'And what can you tell me about Vladivostok fifty years ago?' I asked, trying to bring him back to the reality that interested me.

'It was a completely different situation. Those who passed through here dreamt of disappearing somewhere else. The proximity of the border and the presence of the port always encouraged some to try to escape from communism.'

Suddenly my mind went back to Irina's message. It was clear that in her case she was not trying to flee; Vladivostok was a destination that had been forced upon her.

'The city's isolated position also made it the ideal place to keep troublemakers under control. Do you know how many turned up down here from Moscow?' the Armenian went on, 'but I have a feeling you're here for something else.'

'What do you mean?'

'A woman! I think you're really here for a woman!'

His confident manner took me by surprise.

'It's understandable, sir!' he added, with a wink of agreement. 'Everyone knows Vladivostok is home to the most beautiful women in Russia!'

The Armenian began to pour forth a river of facts and anecdotes about the city, but I could barely follow what he was saying. My attention had focused on something he had said earlier: 'the ideal place to keep troublemakers under control.'

'What an idiot I am that it didn't cross my mind sooner!' I said aloud.

His tone became serious again.

'So? Why don't you tell me, man-to-man, the real reason why you're here?' he added knowingly.

Although he could be unpredictable, his intuition followed a logic that had helped him guess the real purpose of my trip and it didn't make sense to hide the truth from him any longer.

'To find Irina Shestakova!' I answered after a long pause. 'Have you ever heard that name before? Her father was a colonel.'

'No! It's not a surname you hear around here,' he said, coming out from behind the counter.

The conversation with the hotel owner was making me think about something so obvious that it was key: it was easier to control someone in a place located thousands of miles from the capital. The colonel must have thought the same thing when he decided to force his daughter to live as an exile. The idea was consolidating in my mind that the KGB had nothing to do with it and that it was Irina's father who was behind having her sent away.

This theory had already come to me when I reconstructed everything the former commissioner had told me in Aprelevka. The information from the Armenian corroborated the same conjecture.

After all, Irina's parents had never looked favourably on our relationship and her immediate removal to Vladivostok could have represented a move to resolve a very delicate issue which, at first glance, seemed to have a family context, but which, in fact, concerned the colonel's secret military activity.

Every time I rearranged my ideas about the story, the picture that emerged became clearer and clearer: the guys posted in front of the hospital door had to be henchmen in the service of Irina's father and not KGB agents. Their task was to choose the right moment, grab Irina, load her into a suitable vehicle and take her as far away from Moscow as possible, a plan she had evidently sensed and come to reveal to me that afternoon at the hospital.

But who could the accomplices in such a cruel plan have been? Who would be brave enough to agree to the idea of keeping a young woman under control in a completely isolated location? Who could have collaborated with the colonel to make a plan like that reality? Clipping Irina's wings was too presumptuous a request for any colleague, relative or friend in their right mind. Taking her away was a punishment that could only be inflicted with an order that was impossible to avoid. There had to be someone in Vladivostok who was ready to obey the officer's will. An instruction only another soldier or someone trusted could have carried out.

I had revealed the secret I had brought with me from Paris to Russia to the hotel owner. I had done so hoping, in my heart, to get his help in that moment of despair. Before giving up everything and going home, I felt the need to narrow down the field of my absurd search. It was the last attempt and, perhaps, thanks to his help, I was succeeding.

'The colonel must have been a big shot!' said the Armenian after swiftly typing his name into his computer. 'Look, he served in Novosibirsk. Do you know what they were up to on that base?' he asked, his expression changing.

When I thought about it, I did remember that when I was with Irina, I had sensed her father was in charge of an important military project, but I didn't know where. How could I have known? No one was allowed to access such information, not even the family members of those involved.

'The Novosibirsk base has been decommissioned, but they used to carry out weapons experiments in that area.'

With a few clicks, the Armenian had reconstructed the colonel's brilliant career, stressing that for three years he had been the head of a special army department. He even showed me a photo of him in uniform alongside senior Red Army officers. This was another example of the change in Russia, I thought. At the time of the Cold War, it was impossible to publicly access information about military activities.

I explained to the Armenian that these were pure suppositions and not even Irina had known about her father's work. The colonel would disappear from home for two weeks of every month and even when he did come back to Moscow, he would spend most of his time at the Kremlin. The hotel owner listened with great interest. 'Incredible! Your story is really incredible. I admire you greatly, Signor Ceccarelli! I wonder how you managed to travel thousands of miles based on a simple message from fifty years ago.'

'Some impulses come from the heart and can't be ignored,' I answered, thinking about the emotion I felt when I read that note for the first time.

The Armenian had become too involved in my story and you could see that he was itching to help.

'I know Vladivostok like the back of my hand. You can count on me to help find your Irina.'

I lit a cigarette and offered one to my new partner. We

sat down on a sofa in the hotel lobby and began coming up with theories about Irina and what had happened to her.

'He must have relied on a soldier from the fleet,' I said, referring to the colonel.

He shook his head.

'An unlikely solution!' he replied.

'Do you think so? Didn't I tell you that Irina's father was well-known in the military and even had links to naval officers?'

'I don't doubt it. It's just that at that time soldiers in the fleet stayed in quarters inside the port, in a delimited area; believe me, a young woman in there would not have gone unnoticed.'

The Armenian was right. How could somewhere full of soldiers be a hiding place? Even if he'd had a naval officer as an accomplice, the colonel would never have publicly exposed his daughter; it would have been too great a risk. Not to mention that civilians were absolutely prohibited from certain settings. Control over Irina could only have happened in a much more secluded place.

'What if he sent her to work in a re-education institution for minors?' I asked suddenly. 'I don't know, a reformatory or something?'

The hotel owner stood up, went to the window, pulled back the curtain and, looking out, remarked: 'If I understand it correctly, the colonel's aim was to hide his daughter for as long as possible, right?'

'Yes! I would say so.'

'So? Don't you think that would have been too much for Irina to bear? It's good to consider every theory, but even this seems unlikely to me.'

We spent the afternoon going over every clue. The

questions that remained unanswered were always the same: who would have been able to hide a young woman without being noticed? For how long? And again, did the operation to hide Irina involve just one person or several accomplices?

We were getting bogged down. Then suddenly the Armenian's face lit up with an intuition that came out of nowhere. He went back to his computer and quickly typed something.

'In 1963? You said it was November 1963, right?' he asked.

'Yes! But what are you looking for?' I answered curiously.

'Here. Perhaps we've got it! That must be him.'

'Who?' I asked.

'Vladimir Ivanov, the party secretary!'

The Armenian was looking for a possible accomplice for Irina's father in the political rather than military world. For the first time, after a week of fruitless searching, I felt I was moving in the right direction. Of the various assumptions we had developed thanks to his suggestions, investigating the Vladivostok party secretary at the time seemed to me the most convincing. After all, a colonel of Shestakov's calibre was in a position to ask for favours from party members in any city in the country so could have decided to do so to solve the tricky problem of sending his daughter away. The home of the person in question was on the northern outskirts of the city, in a decidedly isolated location.

That was the next step.

...

I went there that same afternoon. Despite the Armenian's willingness to come with me, I decided to go alone. When I got out of the taxi, I found myself in front of a luxurious building, surrounded by greenery. Next to the entrance, near the car park, there was a fountain and a children's playground. A gold plaque on the door showed the words 'The Siberian Hotel & Restaurant'. In a corner of the garden, work tools and a couple of paint tins had been piled up, showing that the work to restore the building was nearing completion. This was confirmed to me by the owner, a young Muscovite who, like other Russian entrepreneurs, had chosen the southeast for his investments. It was he who enthusiastically told me about the project he had just finished: the conversion of an old farm into an exclusive tourist facility.

We had only exchanged a few words when I realised he knew very little about the family that used to live there: 'I'm sorry, sir. I never met the owners personally. The negotiation for the purchase was conducted through an agency. I can only confirm that the house had been uninhabited for some years.'

Once again, I hadn't been able to get the information I had wanted. I had got carried away by the hope of seeing Irina again but had drawn another blank. Despite this, I tried not to take it to heart, nor did I blame myself for refusing to accept it or judge what I was doing too harshly. As even the Armenian had said, if I wanted to find Irina, the only choice available to me was to walk the streets and this was one of many useless and disappointing dead ends.

It was getting late and I decided to hail a taxi back to the hotel. I sat down at a table in the bar to wait for it when new questions about Irina began to haunt me, causing anxiety to rise up in me suddenly. What if Irina really had lived in that house? I wondered. If this was really was where she had been locked up, which room had she spent her days in? And who did she talk to about her desire for freedom, the tenacity and courage I remembered as being among her best qualities? Irina was an impetuous and determined woman and she would never have yielded, out of filial submission or meekness, to an imposition from her father, particularly one so hard to bear.

A lump began to tighten my throat with emotion. I closed my eyes and the image of her appeared once more as it did in my dreams. She was dressed in white and wore her hair tied up in a scarf. 'I didn't do anything and it's not fair to make me pay,' she said. Then nothing more. When I opened my eyes the image of her vanished like a handful of sand in the wind. Meanwhile, a horn announced the arrival of the taxi; I said my goodbyes to the hotel owner and walked towards the exit.

'Wait! Now that I think about it, there is someone who might be able to help you,' he said, accompanying me out.

On so many occasions I had harboured in vain the hope of talking to someone who could put me on the trail of Irina, so I didn't give too much weight to the young man's words.

'Old Igor, who comes in from time to time for a drink. He's gone completely blind, but I can assure you he's still lucid.'

'When would I find him here?'

'As I said, he doesn't come in every day. There's usually a boy who brings him, leaves him for a while then comes back later to pick him up. He's from around here. He'll be able to give you some more details about the house and the people who used to own it.'

A chink of light suddenly appeared in Irina's story. I had the feeling that this old man might be the right person and agreed with myself that I should take the opportunity to meet him.

I had to go back to the bar several times but finally, on 10th August, I had the chance to talk to him. As soon as I walked through the door, the owner signalled to me that he was there; I saw him sitting at a table at the back of the room. I walked towards him, searching for the words to formulate a simple question, the answer to which might finally lead my exhausting search in the right direction.

As I approached, I got a better look at him: he was completely bald and his eyes appeared hollowed out of a map of wrinkles. He was older than me; from what the owner had told me, he must have been in his nineties. He was dressed respectably, wearing a checked suit over a white shirt. I caught a glimpse of a burgundy ascot tie, a rather unusual accessory for a Russian. I noticed the cane hanging from the back of the chair and the hat resting on his lap. He was talking to the waiter, who was busy serving him wine.

I waited for the boy to move away before going over to stand in front of him. Only then did the man raise his head and stare straight into my eyes. I felt slightly awkward; if the owner hadn't warned me, I would never have noticed his blindness. Despite his fixed gaze, I felt as if I was being scrutinised from head to toe. Then, after a brief silence, during which I felt somewhat embarrassed, it was he who broke the ice.

'You've finally come,' he said hoarsely.

His words took me by surprise and I was annoyed at first by what seemed like a joke. I'd never seen the man before: why would he have spoken to me like that?

'There must be some mistake,' I replied annoyed.

'No mistake, Franco. Come, sit down.'

I moved the chair and, without even realising it, sat down beside him.

'Get a glass and pour yourself some wine. It's good, straight from your country,' he added, grabbing the bottle.

'How do you know who I am?' I asked amazed.

'Franco, the Italian, Irina's great love. I know more about you than you can imagine,' he replied as he raised his glass to toast. 'This is an important moment and even if many years have passed, we must celebrate.'

He spoke with little conviction and an expression of sadness across his face. But in that moment, I didn't pay it any mind; the mere fact that he knew who I was seemed enough to rekindle the hope of seeing my Irina again. Someone who spoke to me like that had to be aware of our past. My heart started beating fast; I finally felt as if my search was going to yield the results I was hoping for.

'So, you know Irina Shestakova?' I asked, putting a hand on his shoulder. 'I'm searching for her desperately.'

He put his glass back down on the table and a serious look came over his face.

'Of course! It was right here that I met her,' he answered, throwing his arms wide. 'Now it's been turned into a hotel restaurant, but once upon a time a very important family lived here.'

'How did you know her? May I ask who you are?'

'I'm a music teacher, old and past it now, but that's irrelevant. I told you: I met Irina many years ago when she was living here with the family of Vladimir Ivanov, the powerful party secretary.'

The Armenian's intuitions were correct.

'It was 16th November 1963 when I saw her for the first time. I remember it very well because it was Ivanov's wife's birthday and I was in the house too. I'd been working for them for a number of years by then. They were hard times for a music teacher and, as well as giving piano lessons to their three daughters, I worked as a gardener in the grounds. I spent most of my days at their house.'

'Who brought Irina down here?' I asked instinctively.

'I only found out later, when she began to trust me and decided to tell me about her ordeal. At first, I didn't even wonder. Perhaps it's more accurate to say that I didn't need to know. Despite a certain degree of confidence, there were issues between Ivanov and me into which it was better not to delve and, believe me, Irina's story was one of those.'

'And where is she now? Do you know where I can find her?' Igor went on talking as if I hadn't spoken.

'If we take Ivanov and the colonel out of it, Irina's arrival in this house represented an unexpected event for every member of the family.'

'I asked you where Irina is!'

I repeated the phrase with a more resolute tone and at that point Igor reacted with complete silence. Suddenly the doubt that he was deceiving me came back to torment me. Despite the precise references he had given me about particular details of the past, there was something about his way of presenting the facts that failed to convince me.

What if he was simply reporting events he had been told by someone else? I wondered. Doubts about him began to haunt me. I needed more confirmation to quell my suspicions. Why so many precautions and such a strange reluctance to give me news about Irina's life now? What was the elderly former music teacher hiding? And why?

While, on the one hand, the idea of talking to Igor renewed strength in my heart to continue searching, on the other, his seesawing way of saying and not saying things only generated a feeling of distrust. I needed more information and I couldn't limit myself to listening only to his – perhaps sometimes imaginative – version of when he had seen Irina for the first time. He could have given me irrefutable proof, but that confirmation was slow in coming. It was a detail about Irina that was impossible not to notice. So, to sweep away any doubts, I began asking him about Irina's physical appearance. Only then did Igor make my blood run cold with an answer that silenced my suspicions.

'Do you want to know if I noticed the little birthmark on her cheekbone?' he said.

'Um, no... It's just that.' I mumbled a few words awkwardly.

'Then let me tell you!' he added, before taking another sip of wine. 'It was Ivanov himself who introduced me to Irina. He came in to interrupt the piano lesson I was giving his daughters and said: "We have a guest arriving today." Then he took Lenora, the eldest of the three, to one side and told her: "You are to be responsible for her every move!"

'The first few days were hard for Irina. She locked herself in her room in protest and decided not to come out. Then, as time went on, I was eventually able to interact with her. It was then that she told me about her father sending her away and the three men who had taken her from the hospital.'

'To deliver her into the hands of Vladimir Ivanov,' I remarked.

'Exactly!' he answered.

Igor's confirmation of that detail of her appearance, which Irina had had since birth, helped me trust him more. From that moment on, the conversation between us took a different turn. The change came in my attitude: it was as if I had prepared myself to listen to his words in a different way, at the same time opening myself up to a different view of

Irina's past in Vladivostok. No more imaginative suppositions based on a handful of puzzle pieces, collected in the wrong order. Igor's story reached my ears with credible, targeted, unequivocal episodes and represented the point of view of the only valuable witness I had succeeded in tracing.

We spent the whole afternoon reconstructing the early stages of Irina's compulsory stay in the Ivanovs' house. Her days alternated between moments of profound resignation and peaks of euphoria that were triggered by the dream she continued to yearn for about our future, the hope of seeing me again which, as Igor confirmed, she never gave up on, even at the toughest moments. It was in that context that Irina confided her most hidden secrets to the music teacher. Igor, who was about forty at the time, was kind and helpful to the new guest, which led to the forging and growth of a sincere friendship.

The arrival of a woman like her, young and full of character, somehow changed the harmonious and ordered system of the Ivanov family. From the outset, Irina and her temperament represented a disorderly factor, a gradual and scattered disturbing force, like the waves that spread out across a pond after an object is thrown into it. No one imagined how rebellious a soul she had; no one knew her determination when suffering injustice. The imposition her father had inflicted by forcing her to live so far from Moscow and from me represented too great a wrong not to unleash inside her a combative attitude against everyone. Igor was the only one whom she grew to like and with whom she shared her unhappiness.

Confirmation that the plan for Irina to be moved against her will had been devised and orchestrated by her father had come a couple of weeks after her arrival in Vladivostok.

In a letter to his friend Vladimir, the colonel addressed his daughter with these words: *'You refused to listen to your father's words or your mother's advice. Your obstinacy had to be contained by any means, so that is what I have done. I have put you in a position to think about your behaviour, which has posed a threat to the safety of the whole family for too long. You will be a guest in the house of my friend Vladimir for a while. This is your last chance. You will have plenty of time to think about it!'*

Irina could not bear these impositions, let alone having to be separated from me and live under round-the-clock surveillance. Not that she suffered rudeness or mistreatment at the hands of the family; Igor told me that, at first, both Ivanov's daughters and wife had welcomed her kindly and that Irina was allowed to take part in the same activities as the other girls in the house. She attended piano lessons with them, listened to music, had access to the library, the kitchen and could go into town in the company of Lenora. The youngest of the sisters gave her a puppy so she would not feel alone when she spent entire days locked in her room writing. As time passed, however, the relationships deteriorated; only a month after arriving, Irina attempted to escape. This episode was harshly denounced by Ivanov, who, in keeping the promise made to his friend the colonel, interpreted the gesture as a personal affront. The failed escape attempt provided proof of Irina's courage to all those involved.

'I had already understood how brave she was, but it was with that action that Irina gave me confirmation once and for all. She paid no attention to anything and threw herself headlong into what she believed in.'

'Do you remember what happened?'

'Of course, I remember. She was the one who told me the details of her desperate plan: she went out at night while everyone was asleep and walked to the port area. As agreed beforehand, she met a guy she had got talking to a few days earlier at the market on one of her walks with Lenora. He was a fixer and she agreed with him that he would take her to Khabarovsk by car for a large fee.'

'To Khabarovsk? But that's at least four hundred miles from here!' I remarked.

'Yes. She wanted to go back to Moscow to look for you. Her plan was to travel at night to get to the agreed spot on time. She was planning to continue from there by the Trans-Siberian Railway.'

'And where did she get the money?'

Igor smiled, motioned with his hand for me to come closer and whispered in my ear: 'She took it from Ivanov!'

I gave in to a smile too, which remained imprinted on my mouth, mixed with an expression of disbelief.

'That was exactly what happened! Irina told me she'd rummaged in some furniture in the bedroom and found a bag of roubles. But something went wrong. The fixer kicked her out about a hundred miles from Vladivostok and fled with the money. He disappeared without trace. The following day they found Irina at a service station on the M60 highway; she was exhausted and hungry. Ivanov had used every contact he had at the police station to track her down.'

'It's a miracle she was alive!' I commented.

'Yes! When the agents called to say they had found her, Ivanov breathed a sigh of relief: if it hadn't turned out that way, the colonel would never have forgiven him.'

I was listening intently to every detail of Igor's story when a voice interrupted us: 'I've come to take you home, Uncle,' said a young man approaching the table.

Igor motioned to his nephew to wait, then reassured me by saying that there was more I needed to know and that we could meet the next day at the same time. I was dying to know where Irina had ended up, but decided to go at his pace and accepted the invitation. I had found that he was telling me the truth up to that point and one more day wouldn't change anything. I could wait.

'Don't worry, Franco. I'll tell you everything tomorrow,' he said, holding out his hand.

I returned the gesture and he walked towards the exit, arm in arm with his nephew.

The Wings of Freedom

The Indian politician Jawaharlal Nehru – who used to compare the life of a human being to a game of cards – argued that the meaning of the things we do, as well as of existence in general, does not always reveal itself in the end. Sometimes, the sense of an action appears clear to us even when we can't see all the cards in play. That evening, after talking with Igor, I went back to the hotel with an awareness that, even before finding out what had happened to Irina, I had understood that the journey I had embarked upon was about regaining my true identity. Everything I was experiencing was not just dictated by my heart's need to find the woman I loved; at stake was a process of introspection required so that I could connect with the most intimate part of my being to understand who I really was.

Both the former commissioner in Aprelevka and Igor knew me by my real name. Neither of them knew about the metamorphosis I had undergone to escape the despair of having lost Irina. In truth, that radical choice was also determined by two other reasons: my profound disappointment in the socialist dream I had cultivated and propagated for years and the failure of my relationship with my parents. In all there were three insurmountable obstacles or, at least, so I thought.

It was they, my parents, who sparked in me the desire to leave Italy and disappear forever. In retrospect, I still carry inside me the wounds of the confrontation I had with my mother shortly after returning home from the Soviet Union. The heartfelt story of the misadventures I had lived through in Moscow and the constant sense of a dark force, which had edged its way into the relationship between me and Irina – to the extent that we had been physically separated – had failed to leave even the tiniest of scratches on the wall of the resolute ideology that had been constructed inside my family. Everyone turned their back on me, even my cousin Pietro, who seemed the least aligned with the Soviet orthodoxy. I clashed with people who lacked the ability to form their own arguments, as if they had chosen to live subject to an undisputed faith, placed above all else, even interpersonal relationships. An ideological creed that conditioned every step, every breath, every word.

That afternoon my mother was sitting on the porch writing an article for a party magazine. She had hardly spoken to me for days; my expulsion from the Soviet Union was simply too great a shame for her to absorb and she hadn't wanted to hear my version of what had actually happened. She believed blindly in the official reasons they had formally communicated to me in the expulsion order. She too, like the regime, thought I was solely responsible for the actions that had led to that measure. When I realised there was nothing more I could do to assert my reasons, I decided to let it go.

I left, slamming the door, leaving behind the echo of my mother's blunt and resentful words: 'What do you want me to say, Franco: you had the chance to choose whether or not to stand in defence of the socialist revolution and you decided to betray it! If the Red Army comes, you'll be the first to be shot for destroying our dream with all that talk of the truth. You still haven't understood that *Pravda* is the only truth!'

A few days later I found myself in Paris as a guest at Giovanni's house and I never left.

The question of my identity had re-emerged right in the middle of my search for Irina. I had left Paris as Enrico Ceccarelli, depriving myself of my real name, as if I had forgotten or lost it who knows where. It had been fifty years. I had never considered that only actors on the stage can succeed at these things, not ordinary people perpetually immersed in real life. Only thanks to the abstraction that the theatre can give, and only for the duration of a performance, is it possible to forget who you are and what context you belong to. Even under those circumstances it is a limited experience that cannot last long. At the end of the performance, actors, when they take off their characters, appropriate their true identity once again. And it is to them, as people made of flesh and blood, that the praise or criticism of the audience is addressed. The characters they have just played dissolve behind the curtain and fly away like dust in the spotlight.

In the same way, while on this trip, I stopped identifying myself with Enrico and went back to being Franco. It was as if I suddenly had a feeling of nostalgia for that person who lived inside me, whom I had irrevocably exiled to a small and limited world. Finally, I reflected myself back in my own shadow, from which, by disavowing it, I had removed the right to exist.

...

The next day I arrived half an hour early for my appointment. I wanted to see Irina again so much that I was trembling. Although Igor hadn't yet told me where to find her, something made me think she was nearby. It was not that he had given me any reassurances of that kind, but the aura of mystery didn't bother me too much. If Irina had died, I was in no doubt Igor would have told me.

Before going into the bar, I stopped to look down over Vladivostok from the top of the hill. It looked like a giant nativity scene full of lights and colours, an open-air painting from which I could admire the whole Zolotoy Rog bay. I caught the scent of salt mixed with the spices of a merchant ship that had just arrived from the East. I breathed deeply several times to feel the aroma and vitality of the sea. I closed my eyes and thought about Irina again.

What if she really had died and Igor wasn't brave enough to confess it?

I lit a cigarette and began walking from one side of the entrance of the bar-restaurant to the other, trying to get the idea out of my head. With difficulty, I managed to shift my thoughts to Faustine, feeling a sense of guilt towards her for not having even called once in all the time I had been away. I'd behaved like someone who couldn't give a damn about her completely natural concern to know if I was okay and how the trip was going. I made the decision to call her from the hotel after my meeting with Igor and to tell her, at least briefly, the story about Irina and what had led me to decide to set off in search of her. My mind was elsewhere when I heard the noise of a car a few yards away. It was Igor and his nephew. The young man got out of the car and went around to open the door.

'I'll take care of him,' I said, walking over.

'Who would have thought it?' Igor said, offering me his arm.

I smiled.

'Where did we get to?' he asked.

'To when Irina tried to escape,' I answered as we walked through the door of the bar.

'Oh yes. That time Ivanov was furious and scolded her severely. He called Irina into his study and gave her a final warning: another episode like that and he would tell her father.'

'What happened in the house over the days that followed?'

'From then on Irina lived under day and night surveillance and sometimes it was my turn to keep an eye on her. It was around that time that we became friends. After all, I was the only one who wasn't a member of the family and she realised I was the only one she could trust, just as she was for me!' he added with a sigh.

What did Igor mean by that clarification? Why had he stressed that Irina was the only one he could trust? What secret was he hiding?

'I'll repeat the question,' I said in an irritated tone. 'Where is Irina now?'

He sighed again.

'Why won't you answer me? Is she dead? I asked. 'Tell me if she's dead!'

'No! ... I don't know. I lost track of her a while ago.'

'What do you mean?'

The Wings of Freedom

'That Irina felt hunted like a lion in a cage.'

'I don't understand, Igor. Do you mean she's not in Vladivostok anymore?'

There was a brief silence between us. Then Igor put his hand up to his chin. I looked at his motionless eyes and, in that moment, recognised the serene expression of a man about to reveal the truth.

'Exactly,' he replied softly. 'Irina left many years ago.'

'And where is she now?' I asked.

'In Mexico! That's where you should find her.'

'What do you mean? Is that a joke?'

'No joke, Franco! Irina left the Soviet Union in late April of 1964 after spending more than five months in this house.'

'Are you absolutely sure of what you're telling me? In Mexico? How would she have evaded the control of Ivanov and her father? Not to mention the border. How could she have escaped police checks? It's impossible! Impossible!'

'Of course, I'm aware of the difficulties involved in getting out of the country back then. I remember what life was like in Russia in the Sixties, but I assure you that's what happened. Believe me. I helped Irina Shestakova escape!'

I was stunned by the news.

At first, I felt as if everything I had done up to that point had amounted to nothing and that I was right back at square one after a wild goose chase. But then I was overwhelmed by a mysterious force that urged me to go on and wanted to know the whole truth. I asked Igor to tell me every last detail about how he had concocted the plan.

We talked for a long time and the thing that surprised me most in the reconstruction of the facts was the role Igor had secretly played for years without being discovered. He had been a skilled organiser who had used his contacts to get Irina to safety. But who was this music teacher to get a false passport for a fugitive and devise a series of instructions to allow her to leave the country unnoticed? Who was behind him?

That afternoon I realised Igor had been a person of influence who had chosen to live in the shadows, surrounded by a network of trusted people able to provide support both inside and outside the Soviet Union. The blind old man had a background as someone loyal to a very precise critical and political thought in a way I could never have imagined. It was by observing him from a purely ideological perspective that I was able to understand the reasons behind the extraordinary effort he had made to help Irina. During the course of our conversation, I had to adopt a different interpretation, almost like Sartre suggested with the metaphor of looking down on someone from above: in order to grasp all the characteristics of a man, you have to look down on him from the window of a building.

I instigated a radical change of perspective with Igor to get him to talk. Only then, like a raging river, did he begin to tell me about Irina's adventure.

'When I suggested to Irina the real possibility of helping her, she accepted without thinking twice. From that moment on we began working on the plan. "If you want me to, I can help you escape from here," I told her one afternoon, after our lesson. She nodded. We spent the next two weeks thinking about how to do it, considering all the options, even the most outlandish. Then one morning we put our plan into action.'

'How is it possible that no one in the family became suspicious?' I asked.

'Luckily they didn't. They all trusted me, especially after her first attempt to escape. As things had turned out, Ivanov felt calmer knowing I was the one keeping an eye on his friend's daughter instead of Lenora; he still harboured a grudge against her because she'd failed to watch Irina properly during their trips out of the house. But he never imagined a surprise was coming his way! To begin with, Irina didn't think she would need to go abroad. She was still harbouring the hope of meeting up with you in Moscow and it was there that she had planned to stop off on her journey to freedom. Only then, when she got confirmation that she'd lost track of you once and for all, did Irina understand that there was no time to lose and she had to leave the country: something she did immediately with my help, made indispensable by the circumstances. Consequently, as it was easy to predict, the situation immediately worsened and the atmosphere became too heavy as soon as her father, quickly informed of her escape, began taking steps to find her. I witnessed the telephone conversation between him and Ivanov. The colonel's screams rang out in the room as a clear warning: if the party secretary failed to undertake to find Irina immediately it would have repercussions on his career. And that was exactly how things turned out, but that's a whole other story.'

'Tell me more about Irina,' I said.

'By then, she was already in Moscow, staying with a trusted contact. She had to stay hidden long enough for things to calm down and to get reliable information about what had happened to you. Then, on 27th April, we moved on to the most complicated phase of the plan: crossing the border. In actual fact, there was also another important reason, but I'd like to tell you about that later.'

'Did anyone tell Irina I'd been expelled from the country?'

'No. She knew nothing about what had happened to you. It was as if you'd suddenly vanished into thin air. Your university friends said nothing about you and when my contact tried to reach Giovanni Zampi to get news from your best friend, he found out he was no longer in Moscow either. They had created a void around you. This was the starting point, before anything could be decided about you. Isolating people was the KGB's most tried and tested method. It was then that Irina sensed they had expelled you from the country.'

Igor was right. He was referring to my last spell of hospitalisation when Giovanni, for fear of retaliation, had decided not to return from Austria, where he had gone for a concert. I also experienced the same raw feeling of conspiracy when, following the accident, I found myself in hospital, completely isolated from the outside world.

'My trusted contact in Moscow even managed to access the archive of the medical directorate at the hospital where you were admitted to find out when you'd been discharged. The date coincided with that of Irina's removal to Vladivostok. But you already know all this,' he added.

Igor continued with a detailed account of Irina's final movements, until her arrival in Mexico City in the first week in May. This was confirmed to him by a certain Juan Moreno, the assumed identity of his brother whom no one, including himself until his adolescence, knew existed. From that day on, Igor received no more news of Irina.

'Tell me again about exactly when she escaped. How did Ivanov behave? Were there recriminations?'

'The plan also provided for this risk, but fortunately they believed the only version available. The day Irina left we simulated an assault on me. That morning, Ivanov's wife was the only one in the house. Irina hit me over the head with a bottle and ran away. A car was waiting at the end of the street to take her out of Vladivostok. I let a few minutes pass to give Irina time to get as far as possible and then shouted as loudly as I could. When Ivanov's wife came into the room, she found me half unconscious on the floor with a nasty wound on my forehead. With that set-up I had given myself the perfect alibi, a precaution aimed at diverting any suspicions from me.'

Unlike the Armenian's theories about escaping from the Soviet Union, in Irina's case she did not head east. At the height of the Cold War, the borders with China and North Korea were impassable. Irina's journey to freedom had taken place at the other end of Russia, across the border with Finland, along the 127 state highway north of Vyborg.

Igor told me that the plan had to be implemented by meticulously following instructions Irina carried in the bottom of a bag. These took the form of slips of paper showing a series of places and people to go to in turn for help. In the event of complications, each stage included an alternative plan.

Listening to Igor's amazing story was like watching a film; I could no longer differentiate between fiction and reality. Irina's meeting with the first contact in Moscow seemed particularly audacious.

'Among the instructions I had prepared for Irina, once in Moscow, she was to go to the bus stop in Pushkinskaya Square at precisely midday on 15th April. There she would be approached by a gentleman holding a bunch of red flowers with whom she should go to a nearby restaurant.

The table reserved for the couple was next to that of a guy who, with the excuse of passing the menu, would give Irina fake documents and a note with the address of an apartment in Moscow's southern suburbs, where she was to stay until further instructions. At each stage of the escape there was a confirmation signal that everything was proceeding safely. These were apparently insignificant episodes that Irina had to confirm in order to get the green light for the next phase. Once the instructions had been carried out, she was to burn the piece of paper in question and leave no trace.'

While Igor described the various stages in the escape, I thought about the methods they had employed. They faithfully mirrored the system used by the Secret Services. Even the words he chose were typical of certain environments: instructions, signals, logistics, contacts and safe houses. All this served to pique my curiosity about him even more. For a moment I thought I was looking at an ex-spy.

'How did she manage to evade the border checks?' I asked.

'I prepared a perfect plan!' he replied, with a smug smile. 'Irina arrived in Vyborg by bus and got off near a large wooded area, twenty miles or so from the border. At that point there was a people swap and Irina, along with another fugitive, continued in a vehicle with Finnish licence plates. The other fugitive had also been hiding in Moscow, waiting for the go-ahead. The opportunity arose when a delegation from a Finnish company came to visit the Soviet capital for an important business negotiation.'

'Are you saying that...'

'They posed as someone else!' he finished my sentence. 'Irina and her travelling companion crossed the border with fake documents, posing as a couple of young entrepreneurs, thus avoiding three checkpoints at customs!'

By the time Igor had finished telling the whole story, I couldn't hide the welling satisfaction at its outcome. Knowing that Irina had made it filled my heart with joy, especially because, unlike me, she had reached freedom with a daring escape. The switching of two members of a Finnish business delegation represented a setback for the security of the Soviet regime, even if the episode was immediately repressed and not reported in the press. Of course, if Irina had been caught at the border, the outcome would not have been limited to measures taken against the colonel and Ivanov, and she would have been swallowed up by the jaws of the regime with unimaginable consequences.

By that time, I had been out of Russia for several months and, having lost all hope of seeing her again, had started a new life in Paris with a new identity. Without knowing it, we were both free and in Europe; reality didn't know about us and we didn't know about it, forgetting that you may be able to stop looking for your partner for a while, but you can never stop dreaming of being with them. I had made this unforgivable mistake. I had hastily closed the door on my past and thought I no longer had a way out when it came to surviving life's too many disappointments.

Igor took a sip of water. He too had a satisfied expression on his face, as if by simply telling the story, he had travelled the same journey to freedom.

Igor Smirnov

At two in the morning, I still couldn't sleep. I was tossing and turning in bed, with no idea what to do next. The news I'd received about Irina was out of date and brought the progress I had been making in my search to a juddering halt. It seemed impossible that there was no up-to-date information about her to fill in the gaps of the years that separated us. Everything I had discovered, from the note in her coat pocket to her stay in Vladivostok, dated from too long ago.

Perhaps, as Igor had suggested, the sudden and definitive silence that followed her move to Mexico City was the consequence of the precautionary approach Irina would have needed to adopt to live in peace, a kind of natural instinct that finally allowed her to turn the page. Or maybe not. Igor heard nothing more about her because something had jammed in the mechanism of information that had been arriving regularly from across the ocean up to that point. There was also the critical condition Igor found himself living in after Irina's escape, as well as the fact that he could say almost nothing at all about what had happened. Although everyone officially believed his version, he was put under increasingly intense surveillance. Igor was very adept at not falling into the constant traps the Secret Services set for him and continued working in the house for over twenty years, teaching music to Ivanov's grandchildren. Then, with the fall of the Wall and the then elderly party secretary's loss of power, the atmosphere changed radically. 'Even though I never heard from Irina, one evening I raised a glass to her and toasted her freedom,' Igor told me, just before he said goodbye.

And so, after deluding myself that I would be reunited with Irina in Vladivostok, once again I found myself groping in the dark, drowning in a sea of suppositions. I had to get my thoughts in order to make the right decision about the next step: should I drop everything and go home or take the first flight to Mexico and keep looking for her?

One thing about the story was clear: if Igor hadn't shared Irina's desire to escape from what, despite the lack of bars on the windows, was a prison, he would never have helped her get out of the Soviet Union. The pair, albeit for different reasons, had come together for the escape. While Irina's rebellion may not have been hard to predict due to the inherent difference between her and her father, it remained unclear what had prompted Igor to risk his life to help the daughter of an influential colonel. Who was Igor Smirnov to go against the system? What motivated his incredible tenacity?

Irina dreamt of two things: getting married and going to live in Italy. She loved my country and was fascinated by the Italian language, which, with my help, she had learned with perseverance and commitment. Her ideas were built on the vision of a free world. Hers was therefore a spontaneous reaction to a merciless reality, in the face of which she had put herself on the line, taking the risk of paying dearly for her self-determination. My ideas had shifted from political considerations born of the comparison between my commitment to militancy in Italy and my experience at the university in Moscow. But, unlike me, Irina imagined a model of an abstract society waiting to be discovered.

Like her, Igor did not have a basis for comparison on which to rest the illusion of a world better than Bolshevism. His beliefs had developed through resorting to an ideological mindset he had absorbed like a sponge from an unexpected person: the mysterious brother who had decided, years earlier, to swell the ranks of the exiled.

When I asked Igor who he really was, he revealed his answer with a smile.

'I was a Trotskyist who, unlike plenty of others, decided to stay in the Soviet Union!' he whispered.

Upon hearing that sentence, I instinctively looked around to see if the two guys sitting at the table next to us were listening. For a moment I had lost track of time. Believing the regime was still in full swing, I behaved with the same caution as during the period when saying such things was synonymous with betraying the communist ideology and would have alerted the Lubyanka offices.

'You should have worked it out!' he added.

I had, in fact, worked it out, but I didn't say so. The reference to Mexico had provided an unmistakable supposition that it had something to do with the Trotskyist trail of revolutionaries who had occupied the political stage of the Central American country in the late 1930s. A period of political and cultural unrest that sprang up around one of the leaders of the revolution who, after the split from Stalinism, was accused by orthodox communists of being 'the main enemy of the Soviet Union'. What I hadn't been able to understand about him was how he had succeeded in living a shadowy, almost ascetic life in such close proximity to Ivanov. Or how he had been able to sustain an opposition to Stalinism, remaining perfectly integrated into what, according to the Trotskyists, had turned into a 'degenerate' state, in which the proletariat had been expropriated from political power by the bureaucracy. What I knew about the Trotskyists was what they had instilled in us at the university when teaching Marxist doctrine. In practice, the name had become a label which, after Lenin's death and the internal struggle within the Bolshevik party to choose a new political direction, was used to refer to anyone who had doubts about the Stalinist line. Although Igor was very young in the late Thirties, he remembered the period well.

'It didn't take much to be branded a Trotskyist,' he said with a shrug. 'Those at the NKVD got rid of even the slightest suspicion, even from those who had no sympathy at all with Trotsky. "Everyone who knows must die!" was their motto and, obsessed with threats to attack those in power, they imprisoned thousands of people in the gulags, leaving a long trail of blood and death behind them. I was sixteen at the time and the climate of terror remains imprinted on me like an indelible mark on my skin. From time to time, I happened to hear those who had miraculously escaped talking and I absorbed their way of thinking in all its revolutionary essence. They spoke slowly and quietly, taking care to measure every single word. Theirs was a form of caution, even if to me it seemed like the consequence of a great inner suffering. Some of their stories struck me deeply and one in particular I still remember: it was the case of Ugo Citterio, an Italian who had enlisted in the International

Brigades to fight against the Spanish nationalist forces. After General Franco's victory, he had returned as a refugee to Russia. Citterio was struck by the same fate as other anti-fascists who found themselves in the same conditions and whose passports were seized, meaning they would never be able to leave Soviet soil. He was arrested in June 1940 on charges of Trotskyism and condemned to eight years of forced labour in the Uchto-Izemskij camp, where he died a broken man the following year.'

Igor spoke in a monotone voice, as if he didn't want to let his feelings shine through.

'I'm too old and I no longer have the right to do so,' he said.

In reality, the situation was different: the story of the unfortunate Italian, endowed with incorruptible faith and ideological clarity who, despite everything, ended up falling victim to the system in which he had believed, had marked him deeply. After finishing the story, he paused, waiting for my reaction, but I didn't interrupt. I had decided to absorb his story in one breath.

'Until I was a teenager, I grew up believing that I was the son of an important violinist from Moscow, an illustrious party man, very close to Stalin. Then, suddenly, I learned that I had been conceived out of wedlock and that my biological father was a Trotskyist who had fled to Mexico after fighting in the Spanish Civil War. My mother told me the truth when she found out about his sudden death. My father had been struck down by an illness, depriving me of the chance to get to know him and leaving me only an artificial image I had reconstructed through my mother's few memories. I also found out I had a brother, ten years older than me, the first-born son my father had had with a woman from Kazan.

His name was 'Vladimir,' but he had changed it to 'Juan' on arriving in Mexico. He and my father had fought together for the same ideals, not against the Soviet Union but against Stalin and his tyranny. With that I began analysing political theses, never losing sight of the fact that I was surrounded by people who had a visceral hatred for Trotskyism. This was why I learned to act cautiously, never making mistakes, like a cat in a glass shop.'

'Why didn't you join your brother?'

'I promised my mother I wouldn't abandon her and decided the only way to obstruct the regime was to do so from within. At the same time, my passion for studying music was ploughing the furrow of my destiny, which years later, ironically, took me to Ivanov's door.'

While Igor's long confession had clarified certain aspects of the past, he had also left open a series of questions for which I had not yet managed to find answers. The unsuspected music teacher, like all Trotskyists, was in favour of the idea of expanding the revolution around the world and hoped, at the same time, to be able to live a better future in his own land. With a path similar to mine, he too had based his convictions on ideology, attributing it to the hope of seeing the 'permanent revolution' accomplished. But, unlike me, he had never questioned himself, or so it seemed, even if in his story he hinted at a certain detachment from the past, as if his original ideas had been swept away by the wind of the radical and physiological transformation of Russia in which we had both, at one time or another, believed.

Igor's criticism of Stalinism, after Irina had fled, took shape with the dissemination of ideas contrary to the regime, a strategy he implemented with the help of a network of opponents who shared his goals. To gain access to certain settings, he repeatedly exploited the name of his adoptive father, finding collaborators even among the musicians at the conservatory. These were clandestine acts of counter-information that succeeded in piercing the dense network of Soviet censorship.

Speaking with Igor, I realised that his life as an opponent had taught him many things and the organisation of Irina's escape was just one example of his skills, undoubtedly among the most successful. I paused to think about his characteristics for a while: Igor was like a chameleon, endowed with great intelligence and an extraordinary ability to communicate. I wondered what Irina's mind had absorbed in the months they spent together and how much of his political beliefs she had taken with her. In other words, had Irina accepted Igor's help because she was fascinated by him, while sharing his Trotskyist ideology, or had she exploited the situation simply to escape Vladivostok? The journey that I was facing was motivated by a series of goals, not least in wanting to understand the political choices I had made as a young man. Finding answers to such questions might help me understand if the disappointment I felt towards ideology came from a political maturity reached after my experience in the Soviet Union, or was merely a reaction to my parents' imposition.

Irina's way of thinking, in this sense, was the litmus test of my considerations. To find answers to all this, my only choice was to continue on my journey and hope to find her still alive by following the tracks Igor had given me. I needed to find out about the most clouded part of her story that not even he had been able to clarify for me.

The risk of drawing another blank was great; I had too few clues to help find her and Igor had never heard from her directly, nor from his brother, who had probably been dead for several years, given his age. Looking for Irina in a city of over ten million would not be an easy task. Despite this, I did not lose heart and decided to set off.

Irina had arrived in Mexico City thanks to an escape plan so detailed that it even included a stage for adapting to a new reality. She would be offered logistical and financial help by local contacts, who would provide her with accommodation and enough money to start a new life. In addition to the details of Igor's brother, I also had with me the names of two Mexicans who were supposed to help Irina at the start of her exile.

'How will you find her?' Igor asked before taking his leave with a warm hug. 'It's not going to be easy, my friend!' I didn't reply. Although Igor was absolutely right, I felt as if Mexico City had now taken up a very specific place in my soul. The ten thousand kilometres I had travelled to find out where Irina had ended up had not been enough to allow me to meet her, and as many again were waiting for me.

I continued on my journey and on 15th August, after an interminable flight, I landed at the Benito Juárez airport in Mexico City.

Coyoacán

I stood stock still under the canopy of the taxi stand, holding my suitcase. I looked up to the sky, which was illuminated at regular intervals by the powerful headlights of the landing planes. I stared at the heavy rain. I don't know how long I remained in that position, but I remember the people in line behind me asking to get past. Politely. I could hear their voices in the distance as I continued watching the drops of water bounce off the ground like glass marbles. I felt as if I was living in a world in which the events around me – even something simple, like the rain – seemed to have been slowed down on purpose for me to watch them, experience them. I was in Mexico.

'*Adelante por favor,*' said the taxi rank supervisor. Only then did I take a few steps forward, gesturing to the oncoming taxi to pull over to the shelter to avoid the large puddle that had formed. In the meantime, a child tore the suitcase from my hands and slipped it lightning fast into the boot of the taxi. The driver didn't seem unduly concerned and didn't move from behind the wheel; it was only when he noticed my expression of astonishment in the rear-view mirror that he thought it best to reassure me: 'It's OK… it's

OK, don't worry' he said, reaching out to open the door for me. Before I got in, I looked back towards the child and found myself confronted by two endearing dark eyes. His gaze, deep and intense like the waters of a lake, betrayed the restlessness of someone who had no choice but to grow up quickly, unaware of what a childhood was. We looked at each other for a moment before he came over, holding out his hand, palm up. I smiled at him and he smiled back. A handful of white pearls appeared at his mouth, contrasting with the skin of his face, as dark as damp earth. I took some coins from my pocket and filled his hand. They may have been roubles or euros, I don't remember, but he didn't care: '*Muchas gracias señor. Bienvenido en Mexico*,' he said, hurrying off to grab another passenger's suitcase.

The strange sensation I had felt as I stepped out of the airport would stay with me throughout my time in Mexico City: a state of mind I was only able to put my finger on a few days later. All I can say is that it was an abstraction of the frenetic pace of Paris, in which I'd allowed myself to be caught up and carried away for too many years. It was an almost surreal way of perceiving life, a detail that at the beginning I had hastily considered trivial, but which proved to be fundamental to understanding the 'Mexicanness' into which I had been catapulted to chase after Irina at all costs.

I got into the taxi and said the magic word: Coyoacán.

'I would have bet on it!' exclaimed the driver. 'Someone like you is only ever going to Coyoacán,' he added with a laugh, launching his old Peugeot at full throttle along the Circuito Interior, the never-ending racetrack that surrounds the city centre. I returned the joke with a half-smile, without concealing a veil of satisfaction. Although I'd never been to Mexico City, I knew the fame of that colonial paradise well.

Come With Me

Coyoacán was a pearl of the Distrito Federal to which the bohemian cream of the Mexican capital had flocked since the Thirties. While it was every taxi driver's job to curry favour with their customers, the fact that he associated me with a similar cultural background tickled my ego for a moment. After years teaching the philosophical thought shaped in that city, chance had wanted me to come here in person to sample its flavour for myself. On more than one occasion, Igor had confessed his desire to visit the places where his father and brother had fought alongside those loyal to Trotsky. Coyoacán had generously welcomed refugees like them, who had escaped the purges of the party – they were almost all veterans of the Spanish Civil War.

Here too ideology had claimed its victims and Coyoacán became the scene of political executions, as well as the backdrop for mysterious and risqué love stories between famous lovers. Much has been said about the life and background of the communists in Mexico City at that time and perhaps, in the climate of constant suspicion typical of certain circles, some have even speculated about it. But the fact remains that in the flow of avant-garde thought, individuals would occasionally die silently at the hands of assassins who were careful not to leave even the slightest shadow of evidence. Murders were almost always committed using *curare*, a deadly poison that went undetected by the coroners charged with ascertaining the cause of death, which was too often hastily attributed to a sudden heart attack. Internationally renowned artists such as Diego Rivera, Dolores del Rio and Hannes Meyer had walked the narrow streets of Coyoacán. Someone else who frequented those circles was the Chilean poet Pablo Neruda, who left an indelible mark on Mexican history when, shaken by the sudden death of his actress friend, the Italian anti-fascist Tina Modotti, he wrote a poem that moved the whole world – *Tina Modotti is dead*.

The first of the two addresses I was supposed to go to for information about Irina was 144, Calle Aguayo, a street two blocks from the Frida Kahlo Museum. The guy I was looking for was called Pedro Ramirez, at the time a young musician who had been introduced to the group of artists close to Trotsky by one of his bodyguards. It was just after midnight and, at the suggestion of the taxi driver, he took me to a nearby guest house so I could start looking for Irina properly the following morning. The charming B&B in Calle de Paris welcomed guests with a brightly coloured sign displaying the words 'Violeta del Alma'. It was named after Donna Viola, an elderly Californian singer who had crossed the Mexican border in the early Seventies and decided to stay forever. 'I stopped in Coyoacán because it's a magical place,' she immediately assured me, welcoming me with a smile as she showed me around. 'You'll see that tomorrow when the sun comes out.' At first, I didn't pay much heed to her words. I was tired and rest was the only thing on my mind. Early next morning, all I had to do was take a walk in the Parque de los Coyotes, in the centre of the village, to come to the realisation that I was in an exclusive and entirely intellectual spot, a real island amid Mexico City's sprawl. Another world.

A few hundred yards away as the crow flies, the deafening chaos of the horns of a river of slow-moving cars and the air saturated with carbon monoxide showed the capital's other face: thousands of Chilangos, Mexicans living frenetic lives in the city centre, travelling to and from their places of work.

Along the streets, immersed in an unreal silence, I felt as if I'd taken a leap into the past, to a place where history had planted its roots in every corner. At the same time, I breathed an air of creative vivacity, a feverish cultural renewal compared to dormant Europe. Beautiful murals, sculptures and brightly coloured mosaics were everywhere: red, blue, yellow, green, turquoise, gold and then blue again, in a thousand shades, a chromatic game of too many tones to count.

I went into the garden of the house of the legendary Hernan Cortés and ordered a coffee at one of the patio tables. I lit a cigarette and stared into the lush plants and their colourful flowers, falling prey to the intoxicating scent of age-old tree trunks and ancient civilisations. I glanced inside: the walls dripped with culture like chlorophyll from the huge plant of knowledge that so many thinkers had come from all over the world to water. While I was smoking, I closed my eyes to better listen to the background music that was coming from the still half-empty room at that time of the morning. I thought to myself that there was a similarity between that garden and the bistro I usually visited on my Paris walks: both places acknowledged the presence of special customers, men and women who had left an indelible contribution on humanity. Beyond the ideological manipulations that had influenced their thinking throughout history – a fact that has always represented a true obsession for me – I have to admit that it takes an attitude free entirely of prejudice to fully recognise their merit.

I looked at my watch and made up my mind to leave. I asked the waiter for the bill and, while I waited, had one last thought before leaving Cortés' enchanted garden, the same that had struck me in a Vladivostok tearoom: there is a thread that unites cultured people, a subtle connection through which ideas and emotions travel from one side of the planet to the other. In Paris, as in Mexico City, and every other city in the world, certain places are like small sanctuaries along the way, ideal spaces for sharing knowledge, where the spirit and intellect can be refreshed, spaces that have been created specifically to allow us to continue satisfied along the fascinating journey that is the knowledge of things.

To get to 144, Calle Aguayo I had to walk the length of a red wall. It had faded with time and was almost entirely covered in graffiti and thick layers of posters – a legacy of past events that had never been removed – depicting the faces of candidates from electoral campaigns of the past. Through small grates and crumbling openings created by time and neglect, I could peer through the wall. I realised the address I was looking for corresponded to an old warehouse; the building was in a serious state of neglect and overlooked a yard completely covered with weeds. In one corner lay a van and, a short distance away, a goods lift, both buried in dust and rustily corroded. I continued along the wall and found myself in front of a gate closed by a large chain. A miraculously intact old plaque dangled on a hook. I walked over to read the faded writing and could barely make out the name of that now forgotten place. '*Fabrica de ceramica de Luis Reyes.*'

What did Pedro Ramirez have to do with this ceramics factory? I wondered. Igor had told me about a musician, but the address he had given me corresponded to an abandoned warehouse. What was the connection between the two? I checked the piece of paper again, hoping to have misread the street number, but was forced to accept that this was the right place. Not that I had expected it would be easy to find traces of Irina in Mexico City. The information I'd received about her was from too long ago, but I was hoping, at least, to meet someone I could ask.

I didn't lose heart and walked around the block to see if there was a way into the factory. As I started down the street parallel to Calle Aguayo, I noticed a small door that led straight to the back of the building. It was ajar and unlocked, opening when I gave it a gentle shove. So it was that I found myself inside the old factory. It was in such a state that I thought it must have been looted, a punishment inflicted by way of retribution. Pieces of large ceramic vases, crushed one by one, lay on the shelves arranged along the main wall. The tools, as well as the terracotta moulds, had all been destroyed. The same was true of the kiln, which had been demolished with a pickaxe. Even the cooling tanks had been ripped up from their bases.

I went all the way to the end of the warehouse, where the owner's office had presumably once stood. There too everything had been demolished. The desk and wardrobe had been set on fire, and on the ceiling, partially blackened by the smoke, I could make out some black writing. It must have been the signature of the devastation's perpetrators, but I couldn't decipher the name. Half hidden behind the door was a filing cabinet, some drawers of which had been removed. Instinctively I tried to open one, but it fell to the ground. The crash when it hit the floor rang out so loudly that it scared some birds hiding under the roof. They flew out through a shattered window. The fear that someone outside might have heard caused a sudden wave of anxiety. How would I justify my presence in this abandoned place? The situation was getting risky and I had decided to leave when I realised something had fallen from the filing cabinet. I looked down and saw a pile of partially burnt papers. I picked one up; it was a flyer for the Partido Comunista Mexicano, dated 1976. I said the few words I could read out loud: *'Mexican federal elections. Vote for Campa, the candidate for struggling workers.'*

Once outside, I went back to the main entrance. If I wanted to understand anything about the ceramics factory, I would have to ask someone in the area who was old enough to remember its history. And so I did. Taking advantage of the kindness of Mexicans, I stopped a man about the same age as me and asked for information.

'Yes, sir!' he replied politely. 'Reyes pottery was known all over the country. Its factory was the jewel in the crown of Coyoacán. All the houses around here have something that was made in there,' he said as he pointed to the warehouse.

'And why did it close?' I asked.

The man suddenly turned serious.

'I'm talking about when Luis Reyes was in charge, not his son. It was during the son's time that the factory ceased production in '76. A detail that few people remember today,' he specified.

'Do you mean events linked to the Communist Party?' I asked, showing him one of the flyers I'd picked up.

He looked at it quickly and nodded. Then he explained that Reyes's son was a young communist leader who used to organise meetings with party members from other delegations in the early Sixties. The political activity in his father's factory became more and more intense until it reached its peak on the occasion of the presidential elections of 1976. Despite the considerable success of Campa, the railway unionist who had taken over a million votes, the election had been a joke. At that time the Communist Party was not officially registered in electoral campaigns and votes for Campa were counted as 'null'. My theory that politics lay at the root of the miserable end met by the abandoned factory had been confirmed by the area's elderly resident. I was familiar with the evolution of Marxist-Leninist ideology in Mexico and knew that, with the exception of short periods, the Mexican Communist Party had clashed with successive governments and, in some cases, even been declared illegal. From Igor's story, I learned that his father and brother, exiles in Mexico during the Cárdenas government, had both joined the party, which, at the time, was a jumble of ideologies in which anarchists, Trotskyists, Marxist-Leninists and other revolutionaries coexisted.

El Gordo

My search for the musician had not gone well. All I could do now was try the second contact, a certain Pablo, known as 'El Gordo' (the Fat One), whose last name not even Igor knew. His address was right in the city centre, Avenida 5 de Mayo, near the famous Plaza de la Costitución.

Keen not to waste any time, I decided to go there that same afternoon. I could hardly believe it when the taxi driver showed me the address; it was the entrance to a typical Mexican cantina. The smell of freshly fried tacos wafted out of the place, tickling the taste buds of the tourists passing by. The cantina must have been one of the oldest in the city, a place where devotees would go to worship at the altar of traditional Mexican cuisine. This was confirmed to me when I read the year in which the cantina had opened, engraved on a marble plaque at the entrance for all to see: 1931. The rusty sign said: '*El Rey del Chicharrón*'.

I walked over to the entrance and peered inside: it was full of people drinking, shouting and playing dominoes. The waiters darted from table to table taking orders. Every time they went back to the kitchen, they would take an impressive number of empty beer and tequila bottles, which they managed to balance on giant trays. Every now and then the collective chatter would be overwhelmed by the din of tequila shots being slammed on the table then swallowed. Some would try to mitigate the power of the alcohol by mixing it with soda or drinking it after biting a lemon; the more daring would numb their mouths with a handful of salt.

I walked in and began wandering among the tables when my eye was caught by a host of memorabilia in a display case. It contained everything you could possibly imagine: books, liquor bottles, leather items, cigar boxes, pieces of silverware and old photographs. A sombrero, a rifle and two knives had been hung on the wall in one corner of the room. A sign informed the curious that the relics had belonged to Rosario, a fighter loyal to Emiliano Zapata during the Revolución.

I found myself in front of the counter, unwittingly hindering the comings and goings of the waiters. 'Sir, you have to order at your table,' a girl told me in a scolding tone while filling tacos. I didn't answer. The idea of asking for El Gordo made me feel ridiculous and I thought twice about formulating the question. Asking for a guy who could only be identified by the most common nickname in the Hispanic world was daunting and I was already mentally prepared to suffer another failure in my search for Irina.

A different waiter asked me to get out of the way. This time I managed to ask the question:

'I'm looking for El Gordo. Do you know where he is?'

The waiter looked at me for a moment without saying a word, then, pointing to a tray on the counter, asked the girl: 'Is this for Table 8?' She confirmed. His complete indifference towards me made me doubt that I had sounded sufficiently convincing. I was wrong. 'He's in the kitchen! Ask the girl to call him for you,' answered the waiter, before disappearing off into the crowded room, rudely batting away the salacious jokes aimed at him by the customers. I followed his advice.

When El Gordo peered out to see who was looking for him, I understood the reason for the nickname. A colossus – well over six feet tall and imposing in size – appeared before me. He was hot, wearing a sauce-smeared kitchen apron with his shirt sleeves rolled up to the elbows of his almost completely tattooed arms. My first impression was that he was a gentle giant, ready to turn into a volcano if anyone took advantage of his good nature. He exchanged a few words with the girl then walked towards me; I'd taken a seat at the only free table. He came over, holding out his hand, and said: 'I'm El Gordo.'

Instinctively I stood up, trying to reduce the difference in height a little, but the result was almost the same.

'My name is Franco Solfi and I need to talk to you,' I said, returning the greeting.

'And what does an Italian with a French accent want from me?' he asked.

That detail was enough to trigger a suddenly cautious approach towards me; I knew it from the way he released my hand. As I had the chance to check later, the mismatch between the presumed nationality of my name and the one easily deduced from my pronunciation had reminded him of a great many exiles who came to Mexico to rebuild a life in hiding. I ignored it and continued.

'I'm looking for a woman… Her name is Irina.'

El Gordo remained impassive. I immediately realised I had made a meaningless request. How could he have known Irina by her real name? She had got out of the Soviet Union by posing as someone else to get across the Russian-Finnish border using a fake passport belonging to an employee of a company in Helsinki. Not even Igor knew the name she had taken on arriving in Mexico City.

'I don't know any Irina,' he replied succinctly.

Once again, I sensed a brusque attitude. So I tried to be more direct.

'Igor Smirnov told me about you.'

'I'm sorry, that name means nothing to me either.'

'But you should know his brother, Juan Moreno.'

Only then did El Gordo change his attitude.

'Come with me!' he said in a serious tone, quickly taking off his apron and leaving it on the counter.

We left the cantina through the service door, crossed the small courtyard of an old building and immediately found ourselves in his home. He invited me to sit on the sofa, took out a bottle of tequila and poured a drink.

'It's quieter here. Please tell me what you meant.'

'It was Juan's brother who sent me. He gave me your name and that of a Pedro Ramirez. He told me the two of you would be able to help me find Irina.'

'Pedro...' El Gordo repeated, allowing an imperceptible veil of sadness to creep into his voice.

'I've already tried to track him down, but I didn't get anywhere.'

El Gordo downed the tequila before refilling his glass and draining it in the same way. His eyes darkened.

'The people you just mentioned are old acquaintances and I can assure you some memories aren't pleasant to remember,' he said, his voice cracking with emotion.

'I knew both Juan and Pedro because they lived in my neighbourhood. Juan was older and like a big brother to me. He had fought in Spain and whenever he would tell us about it, Pedro and I would dream of having an experience like that one day. We would listen, captivated by the tales of his exploits with the republican militias against Franco's soldiers. He was a nostalgic type and sometimes told us about his childhood memories of Russia, of dreams and jaunts in the snow. Then he would tell us about being exiled with his father and how his passion for politics came about. When he drank, he would talk about personal matters, like the time he revealed to us he had a brother he'd never met.'

'Wait, slow down a little. You and Pedro were the same age and you were involved in politics together?'

'Yes, we were barely teenagers. We were the children of workers, aware from an early age of the struggle we would have to undertake. We followed the adults to meetings and, even if we didn't always understand their speeches and strategies, we were well aware of which side to take. We experienced many years of militancy, unauthorised demonstrations and clandestine gatherings that were almost always held in Coyoacán, in a ceramics factory.'

El Gordo told me about his commitment to the party until the factory's closure in 1976 and Juan's sudden death in 1965. He also told me about Pedro's decision to go to Nicaragua in the late 1970s to take part, with his fiancée, in the FSLN's struggle against the regime of the dictator Anastasio Somoza Debayle. A journey from which the Mexican musician never returned. Immediately after remembering Pedro Ramirez, a moment of silence fell in the room and El Gordo's gaze drifted: perhaps he was still chasing the vivid images of his late friend.

I listened carefully to every part of his story, trying to put the information in order like pieces of a jigsaw puzzle. El Gordo had also lived through an adolescence as a militant and he too, in his own way, had been a 'pioneer'. I wondered if he had remained faithful to ideology throughout his political career or had felt the same disappointment as many and camouflaged himself in society to hide his personal torments. Although he didn't ask, I began to tell him about my journey: my commitment to the Communist Party in Italy, my experiences in Moscow, the university, my love story with Irina and my expulsion from the socialist homeland, the last act of that sad experience, the final parenthesis of one, yet significantly relevant, part of my life. I was curious to know if there was an analogy of this kind between us.

'What's left of that past?' I asked.

'Our problems were different. Here, communism had to deal with the party's internal contradictions and inconsistencies. This affected its ability to play a role in the political life of this country. Ideological positions were gradually replaced by the opportunist and deceptive theory of progressivism, the mortal enemy of the working class. Do you know who benefited from all of this? The PRI, who have been in government for over sixty years, with their neoliberal policies.'

El Gordo spoke with a knowledge of the facts and used an agitated tone of voice, perhaps due in part to all the tequila he had been drinking. It didn't take much for me to realise that the word communism was still part of his militant vocabulary. Despite the party's recurring crises, he had remained a staunch Marxist and, from the way he spoke, had not lost hope of seeing the socialist dream come true in a profoundly changed Mexico. I would have liked to continue our political discussion, but it was getting late and I still hadn't found out anything about Irina. We resumed talking about her.

'You must care a great deal about this woman!' observed El Gordo.

What do you think? I've been travelling for more than a month without stopping, even for a moment and I don't intend to do so until I find her, dead or alive. If I'm here, it's because I hope you can help me find her... and possibly alive.'

'Don't worry! Tell me what you want to know.'

I rearranged my thoughts and told him everything I knew about Irina's escape: 'In April 1964, Igor Smirnov helped a twenty-three-year-old woman flee the Soviet Union. The plan also included the collaboration of his brother Juan, who was supposed to provide support for the young woman once she arrived in Mexico City. Please try to remember! The woman I'm looking for was my fiancée and the daughter of Colonel Shestakov, an important officer in the Red Army.'

El Gordo let his mind wander and began digging back into his memory. We remained silent. The only noise was the distant shouting of customers coming from the cantina. Then, illuminated by a sudden memory, he looked into my eyes in a firm voice and said a name: 'Ester Montoya!'

'Who?' I asked immediately.

'The woman you're chasing!' he answered ironically.

'Why? That is what you're doing, isn't it?' he commented a little caustically.

'You've crossed an ocean and visited countries on two continents to find her. I wonder how many men your age would have been as persistent for a woman.'

I wanted to avoid yet another disappointment and tried to contain the feeling of relief I felt at that moment. Despite everything, a thrill of joy ran through my body: perhaps El

Gordo really had realised who Irina was. He seemed like an honest guy and certainly had no reason to invent a name.

'Are you sure?' I asked, instinctively grabbing him by the arm.

'Yes! Without a shadow of a doubt. I picked her up at the airport. I remember she was travelling on a Finnish passport.'

'Finnish? You said Finnish?'

'Yes! Her name was Ester Laine. She spoke good Italian and that left an impression on me.'

'It was her! It was her!' I exclaimed. 'Igor told me about the border with Finland. And Irina loved Italian back then. She learned it from me. Please tell me where I can find her.'

El Gordo got up.

'I'll be right back,' he said, going into the other room. A few minutes passed and while I waited, trembling with anxiety mixed with a vague sense of fear, I decided to take a look at the bookcase behind me. As well as essays on Marxist theory and the main works of the members of the Frankfurt School, there was a large collection of books by South American writers. The complete literary works of Carlos Fuentes, Octavio Paz, Julio Cortázar, Pablo Neruda and many others were preserved in strict order. The covers of some of the books had worn over time. I picked one up. It was a collection of poems by José Emilio Pacheco. I opened it and read one, called *After everything*.

> *Where did what happened end*
> *and what became of so many people?*
> *As time passes, we become*
> *more and more unknown.*
> *Not even a sign of our loves*
> *is left in the trees.*

> *And friends always leave.*
> *They are travellers on the tracks.*
> *Even if one exists, for others*
> *only loneliness counts when*
> *it comes to telling her everything*
> *and facing up to it.*

I found myself confronted by a poem on the theme of loneliness, a difficult dimension I had accepted as a new existential state after losing Irina. My attention was drawn to the last sentence: *'telling her everything and facing up to it.'*

That was the real reason for my search.

'Ah! You're browsing through the labyrinths of my ideological thought,' El Gordo said, referring to his books as he came back into the room.

'They're in that state because they were leafed through a thousand times, back in the good old days when I was committed to politics.'

El Gordo was holding an album of photographs from the period relating to his long militancy. He began looking through it, making passing comments about individual photos. Every now and then his gaze would linger on some of them nostalgically. A short pause and then he would start again. Suddenly, he took a photograph from one of the pages, glanced at it quickly and showed it to me. The image depicted a group of people in workwear.

'Look carefully at the fourth woman from the right,' he said.

I counted the people, moving my gaze along their faces until I was confronted by Irina. Suddenly, I felt a lump in my throat and my heart surged in my chest with emotion. The unexpected heat brought sweat to my forehead. I tried to speak but my vocal cords were broken and I couldn't say anything. Without taking my eyes off Irina, I poured myself half a glass of water to clear my throat and settle my emotions. I took a sip.

'So? Is that her?' El Gordo asked, with a half-smile of condescending satisfaction.

'Yes!' I replied, with my heart in turmoil. My hands still trembling with emotion, I wiped my sweat-beaded forehead.

San Miguel de Allende

Finally, persevering in my search for Irina was giving me the results I had hoped for. The vague answers I'd had until now suddenly seemed to have vanished. El Gordo had worked with Irina for five months at the Reyes factory before losing touch with her when she quit her job to enrol at the university. The photograph I found myself holding had been taken in the factory yard; I recognised the same van I had seen when I was exploring Coyoacán in the background.

Irina was between two women who were posing and smiling for the camera. She, on the other hand, had a serious expression and was looking at the ground. Amid the group of workers was Señor Reyes, the only one wearing a jacket and tie. Next to him, I caught a glimpse of Pedro, inseparable from his guitar as always. El Gordo had told me that during breaks from work he would strum to relieve the tiredness, defuse the tension and raise spirits. He would sit on a chair in the middle of the warehouse and play folk songs by Chavela and Antonio Aguilar that he had learned from his father, a famous *ranchero* musician.

'It was at the start of Ester's time in Mexico City,' El Gordo specified. 'Then I never saw her again.'

'Why did she leave? Did something happen?'

'No. Ester was just different...'

'What do you mean? Please tell me what you mean.'

'Well, she was quiet and preferred to be alone. After work, while the rest of us would all meet up at Pedro's or some other workmate's house, she would stay in her tiny apartment, spending hours reading. She understood that factory life didn't satisfy her ambitions. Not that she wasn't a good worker. She was reliable, very scrupulous and got on well with the other workers.'

'So?'

'One day she decided to leave.'

'Yes, you said that. Because she wanted to go to university. But why all the mystery about her. Can you tell me who Ester Montoya is?'

El Gordo smiled. He walked back towards the bookcase and took down another book. 'Here's the answer to your question!' he said, handing it to me. I took the book from him. It was entitled *The Leap* and on the bottom of the cover it read: 'a novel by Ester Montoya'.

'Your Irina is a very popular Mexican author.'

I looked at El Gordo in disbelief. But the idea that Irina had started writing intrigued me. I smiled, thinking about how far she had strayed from the life-plan she dreamt of when we were together in Moscow. 'I want to be an architect because they give shape to the land,' she confessed to me one evening in a bar. But instead, this...

'Look, I've got everything she's ever written,' continued El Gordo. 'Her novels are incredibly steeped in reality, crazy stories but ones we experience every day here in Mexico. Montoya knows how to express the feelings of joy, sadness,

San Miguel de Allende

sarcasm, hope, anger and fear we Mexicans have. Pick one and read it, only then will you see what I'm talking about.'

I hesitated in taking it.

'Come on! It's a gift!' he added.

'Thank you. But I'll take this one if you don't mind,' I replied, referring to *The Leap*, which I was still holding.

'Great choice! It's the last one she wrote.'

'But it's from eleven years ago!' I noticed, reading the publication date on the back cover.

'I know, she hasn't written for a while,' answered El Gordo.

'But is she still alive?' I asked impulsively.

'Well, I can assure you that if she'd died, the news of her death would not have gone unnoticed.'

I breathed a sigh of relief.

'Where is she now?'

'She moved to San Miguel de Allende, in the state of Guanajuato, a lifetime ago. It's about three hundred kilometres from here. She left Mexico City in the mid-1970s after her marriage to the actor Carlos Montoya. He was from that area and they decided to move there.'

That was how I found out Irina had got married. Although the news was entirely predictable, it was a strange feeling. I sensed a pain rise up in me. It was as if I had permanently lost something that, although part of a distant past, I still felt belonged to me. On a rational level, that sudden thought was nonsense, I know, but how often do we feed our convictions without realising it? The idea that Irina had lived a lonely life, as I had, was one of those. Instead, she had managed to forget me and rebuilt a life with Carlos Montoya, an actor she had chosen as her husband, from whom she had borrowed his Hispanic surname to blend in with another identity.

'Why are you talking about him in the past tense?' I asked.

'Because he's dead. A few months after the wedding he crashed into a lorry on the Paseo de la Reforma. The newspapers had plenty to say about it when they found out he'd been drink-driving.'

We talked a little more about Irina until one of the waiters who was frantically looking for El Gordo knocked on the door. Two lowlifes in the cantina had been overdoing it and, fuelled by the alcohol, were taking it out on each other. Our conversation ended there. I thanked El Gordo for the help he had given me. *'Suerte!'* he replied, squeezing me in a hug before returning to his domain.

In Mexico, Irina had transformed herself into Ester Montoya, a famous writer. In addition to everything El Gordo had told me, there was a huge amount of information out about her online. I looked myself that evening, back at the B&B. Among the many articles, I found an interesting post dedicated to her on a forum about Mexican fiction:

After a few months working at the Reyes Ceramics Factory in Coyoacán, Ester made the decision to enrol at the university to become a journalist. In that context, she developed her original form of social and civil commitment, paying increasing attention to the political life of Mexico. She had links to movements that were active in the squares and moved in cultural circles. After university, she worked for feminist and left-wing newspapers, living out her commitment in a way that was free of dogmas and schemas pre-modelled on visions related to the parties' destinies or actions. She became one of the ideological protagonists, not in

San Miguel de Allende

a Marxian sense, of the youth protest movement. She supported the student rebellions and took part in the demonstration of 2nd October 1968, an event infamous around the world as the Tlatelolco Massacre.

In 1990, Ester Montoya dedicated her tenth novel entitled No Doubt to this painful episode in Mexican history. Her long career has seen her write some fifteen novels: The Butterfly No Longer Flies Alone (1972); Only on Thursday (1973); Be Brave Pedro (1976); The Blue River (1978); The Fisherman of Cruz de Huanacaxtle (1979); This is Nothing (1981); Doña Rosamaria (1984); La Vaquita (1986); Strings of Pearls (1989); The Alleyway (1992); Indolent Tijuana (1996); Narco Marco (1999); Queen Calafia (2002); and The Leap (2004).

Ester Montoya is a consistent, uncompromising militant with a great inner strength. A woman who has breathed in the dust of Mexico's streets and who has always tried to understand the reality into which she fell more than fifty years ago. An author who, before embarking on a career as a writer, was able to deeply internalise the flavour, character and very essence of this country.

I was speechless. The article about Irina gave me back the image of a woman who was steadfast and aware. Unlike me, who for years had been on a tortuous path to try to interpret the meaning and consequences of the abuse of ideology, Irina had managed to grasp the difference between that and politics. Firstly, with her militancy and then with her writing, she had succeeded in undergoing an internal conversion, which served to achieve full political and spiritual maturity, in a secular sense.

I finished reading and was reminded of a consideration by Sartre that one of my students had exposed brilliantly. Although I didn't share the French philosopher's thought entirely, I could only agree with him when he argued that understanding the context in which one lives always implies a process of inner transformation. 'Change the world by changing yourself!' was the conclusion of his argument. Irina had succeeded in doing this by resorting to a particular type of committed writing that, at the same time, rebelled against all forms of injustice. An attitude that fundamentally reflected her character. She had been like that ever since I had known her: her determination to go against her father, an example of someone adamant and reactionary, had forged her politically and predisposed her to unconventional behaviour. Mexico had then developed her sensitivity to social issues.

...

17th August 2015

We were still fifty kilometres from San Miguel when the coach driver pulled into a dirt clearing alongside Autopista 57 to make an unscheduled stop. Two American tourists, sitting at the back, had asked if they could get out to take a couple of pictures. They wanted to immortalise the surreal-looking landscape we were entering, an immense space, subdued by a generous light, full of reflections and shadows. It was the most evocative part of the plateau, where the jacarandas gave way to cacti and countless succulents with golden yellow flowers. The sun was almost setting and a soft, fragrant wind had begun to blow, occasionally allowing us to glimpse the flavour and presence of the pre-desert landscape that was becoming clearer as we proceeded north. The driver agreed to the girls' request despite contravening the transport company's strict regulations. I don't know if he did so out of kindness or because he had been seduced by the luminous beauty of the two Californians. Someone who travelled that route regularly and knew the driver well remarked that he only did it so he could smoke another cigarette before arriving at his destination. Fortunately, our enforced stop didn't last long. We soon resumed our journey towards San Miguel, where we were expected to arrive in half an hour.

I stared at the horizon from the window as I counted the minutes on my watch. I was travelling the final stretch of my journey that separated me from Irina. El Gordo had provided me with the certainty that she was still alive and, considering her fame, it shouldn't have been difficult to find her in the small colonial town.

After I got off the bus, I walked along the cobbled streets of the centre, only then understanding why Irina had chosen to live in San Miguel. Absolute peace reigned there, an ideal condition to take advantage of the silence and listen to your deepest inner voices. An atmosphere coveted by any writer or artist in search of inspiration. Where do the noises go in this town? I wondered. There wasn't the din that there is in large cities; no shouting, no car horns or the roar of aeroplanes. The only sound was a backdrop of jazz music coming from a small bar. A calm and orderly life flowed slowly like the water of a huge river, in which I allowed myself to be gently carried away. San Miguel seemed like a little corner of paradise, a magical place to be savoured calmly, like a good *vino tinto*. The centre, among houses painted warm iridescent colours, tiny craft workshops and typical Mexican chapels, was home to the majestic church of the Parroquia de San Miguel Arcángel, the city's most important symbol. I stood looking at it for a few minutes, impressed by its shape and golden hues.

The story of the construction of the façade was described

on a sign in the atrium. Local self-taught architect Zeferino Gutiérrez had been commissioned to restore the building; his work was inspired by the Gothic style of European churches, in Italy in particular, which he had only had the opportunity to admire from picture postcards.

I asked for information about Ester Montoya from an artisan near the square.

'Ester? Who doesn't know her? You can't go wrong, sir. She lives three blocks from here, in a red house at the end of Correo S.to Domingo,' he said, coming out of the shop to make sure I had understood the directions. The kind and friendly tone the man had used to refer to the author made me realise how much Irina must be loved by her now fellow citizens. For confirmation, I asked the same question to a man sitting on a bench. On hearing the name Ester Montoya, he had the same reaction: 'She came to San Miguel several years ago and immediately became one of us. We're all very fond of her here.' The guy also told me that once, after one of her novels had won an important literary prize, the author's house became a place of pilgrimage for admirers, who flocked to sing her praises and have a copy of her book signed.

Before going to Irina's, I took a room at the Puertecita, a tiny hotel furnished in perfect colonial style a few yards away from Correo S.to Domingo. The time it took to leave my suitcase, have a quick shower and shake off the fatigue and I went out again. I walked along the street, dimly lit by the rickety lights of old street lamps and, in a few minutes, had arrived in front of the red house. It was understated and elegant, enclosed by a small garden. A flight of steps led up to the front door. Knowingly breaking every rule of good manners and privacy, I went to a window, put my face to the glass and peered inside. I couldn't see anyone, even if I could sense the presence of someone in the other room.

I was about to reach the culmination of my journey, the final scene of a show I had never been able to imagine in my head. Suddenly, strange sensations I could no longer control began to erupt in me. How would Irina react on seeing me?

I was dying to see her and hug her again. I closed my eyes and even thought I could smell her perfume. I was there; I could do it. All I had to do was call her.

'Irina… Irina… Irina…!'

I shouted her name three times, abruptly interrupting San Miguel's enchanted silence. A dog began to bark in a garden opposite, attracting the attention of a passerby. The man came over to ask why I was standing in front of the house of the famous writer. 'Can I help you?' he asked. I nodded that everything was fine and he left. From behind the window of a different house someone shouted '*¿Que te pasa hombre?*'

Within a matter of seconds, I had created such a fuss that it would have been impossible not to notice. Immediately, someone in the Montoya house turned on the outside light and came out to see what was going on.

A woman in her forties opened the door. She was not particularly tall, thin, with short hair and dark skin. She was wearing a long floral skirt with a denim shirt. The resemblance to Irina was incredible.

'Who are you?' she asked firmly.

I don't know why, but at that moment I didn't answer. Something got stuck in me and my intention to ask for information about Irina vanished.

'Please tell me what you want?' the woman said again,

pulling the door to the house closed behind her to stop me from peering inside.

'I'm looking for someone,' I stammered unconvincingly.

That idiotic answer was enough to push the situation over the top. The woman's icy stare made me understand.

'Please go away! Don't make me call the police.'

'No, wait!' I begged in a whisper. 'Let me explain. You must be... Ester's daughter, right?'

I hesitated for a moment to call Irina by a different name, while the woman continued glaring at me.

'I told you to go away!' she repeated, raising her voice.

'Don't be afraid. I'm an old friend of your mother and she might be happy to know that I'm here. I've travelled halfway across the world looking for her. Please, let me talk to her.'

'My mother is going through a very difficult time in her life and she has decided not to speak to anyone anymore. Do you know how many loyal readers come here asking about her? I'm sorry, you have to leave now,' she replied, moving back towards the door.

'But I'm not one of them. I didn't even know she was a writer until yesterday.'

She fell silent for a moment.

'So, who are you then?'

'I'm Franco Solfi.'

The woman's eyes widened in amazement. It was enough for me to grasp from her expression that she was aware of my existence. She brought both hands up to her face:

'Franco!' she exclaimed. 'You're Franco?'

'Yes, I am,' I replied.

Without further ado, she went back into the house, leaving me outside with the door ajar. She returned soon afterwards.

San Miguel de Allende

'Come in!' she said in a peremptory tone, showing me the way. 'I've sent my children to their rooms so we can talk freely.'

'Thank you.'

'Forget the thanks. Doesn't it seem inappropriate to you to show up after all this time?'

'It's a long story. I'm ready to tell you if you'd like to…'

The woman's attitude was unfriendly. She had remained standing and was fidgeting nervously. You could see that my presence bothered her terribly.

'Can you tell me your name? I asked.

'Maria!' she said hastily. 'I know your story, my mother told me everything. Many years ago, when I was barely able to understand what it meant to suffer for love. It's incredible. You've got some nerve coming to this house!'

'Please calm down, I'll explain everything.'

'There's precious little to explain! When my mother tried looking for you, she found nothing at all. It was like a stinging pain; she suffered huge torment, enduring the anguish of the darkness that overwhelms love. Do you understand that things like that cause suffering not even a lifetime is enough to make up for?'

'Wait. It's not my fault. They threw me out of the Soviet Union almost overnight. I tried every way possible to get in touch with her, but I couldn't. What else could I do?'

'I'm talking about when my mother came to Italy to look for you!'

'To Italy?' I asked in amazement.

'Exactly. She went to Rome, to your parents' house. They didn't even know what had happened to you.'

Silence fell in the kitchen. A cold shiver seemed to run through the walls. The reprimand for not having been there when Irina had tried to find me weighed down like a stone on my conscience. Maria spoke with the same grit as her mother and couldn't forgive my behaviour.

I explained to Maria that my decision to change my name came only from my desire to break ties with a life that had by then turned its back on me once and for all. Irina, my parents and my passion for politics were all that had filled my life until I was twenty-five, when I thought I could conquer the world. Instead, like pillars of cardboard, my dreams had collapsed one after the other within the space of just a few weeks. The loneliness, aggravated by increasingly dismal thoughts, refused to leave me in peace: at night it exposed me to the most terrible nightmares and during the day it made me cry, tormenting me with visions of death.

'Do you believe me now?' I asked, staring into her eyes.

'It was my friend Giovanni who saved me from the decision to take my own life. In a moment of depression, I even considered that extreme solution. I moved to Paris to invent a new life and rebuild my surroundings, without even knowing what had happened to your mother.'

'Why are you lying to me? Why are you pretending you didn't know they'd taken her to Vladivostok?' she asked.

Maria was becoming confused. Who knows what Irina had told her to make her continue accusing me of not telling the truth? We had been talking for about an hour and she had asked so many questions without giving me the opportunity to give my side of the story.

'Vladivostok? I only found out that they'd sent her down there a month ago. That's why I set out to find her and have only managed to track her down now.'

Silence fell again.

Maria's expression changed. She closed her eyes, took a

San Miguel de Allende

deep breath and swallowed. Then, in a broken voice, asked: 'Only a month ago?'

'Yes. I was tidying up my cellar and I found her note.'

I went on to tell her about my sudden decision to leave for Moscow. Maria continued resting her hands on the table. She lit a cigarette and, without even asking me if I smoked, offered me one. She pushed the chair back and finally sat down, letting her body become more relaxed. She smoked distractedly and listened to the long story of the twists and turns that had led me to Igor. Then I told her about my decision to come to Mexico, and my decisive encounter with El Gordo.

'My mother was convinced you'd read her message. She didn't know that two Secret Service agents had come to take you just before she left the note in your pocket.'

It was past one in the morning when I finished telling her the details of everything that had happened up to that moment.

'Can I see your mother now?' Maria's eyes darkened.

'My mother isn't here,' she replied, with a frown.

'Did something happen?'

'She hasn't lived in this house for six months.'

'Where is she?'

'I'm sorry. I haven't stopped crying for days,' she said, drying her eyes with a handkerchief.

'Where is she?' I repeated the question.

'In a clinic just outside San Miguel.'

'Why? What's wrong with her?'

Maria hesitated for a few moments, as if to protect me from bad news. Then, when there was nothing else she could do, she answered:

'She has Alzheimer's.'

El Descanso

18th August 2015

San Miguel was still asleep when Maria picked me up from the Puertecita in her car. I had asked to visit Irina and she agreed. We spent the whole of the short journey in silence. She drove along an isolated road outside the city as I let myself be enveloped by a thousand questions about the illness that had struck Irina. I remembered that one of the neighbours in my apartment building in Paris was suffering from Alzheimer's. Every time I ran into someone from his family, they would tell me about the symptoms that were becoming increasingly subtle and invasive. Maria said the same about her mother. Perhaps she wanted to warn me about her condition.

    We arrived at the El Descanso Clinic car park. Both because of its name and location, the clinic was a real oasis of peace. It wasn't hot yet; the sun was still low behind the trees and the air was fresh and clean. Some of the patients were having breakfast with one of the nurses in the tranquillity of the garden next to the entrance.

    'Could she be with them?' I asked Maria.

'No, she has breakfast in her room with Fernando, the only nurse she gets on with.'

We got into the lift; Irina's room was on the third floor.

'The doctor has prescribed a new drug for her,' Maria said to break the silence. 'It's supposed to be more effective.'

'How is she?' I asked.

'It depends on the day. Sometimes my mother seems like a normal person, but other times she gets everything confused: objects, people, the concept of time. I find it really hard.'

Maria's pupils had widened in anguish and she could barely get the words out without crying. Instinctively I put a hand on her shoulder.

'Can she still write?' I asked.

'She stopped a while ago, although I found a piece of paper in her drawer. She had written a poem in moments of lucidity.'

What a paradoxical situation, I thought. Irina, who had spent her life using her imagination, had fallen victim to an insidious disease capable of delving into the labyrinth of her thoughts and annihilating her memories. I couldn't understand how her destiny could have been turned upside down, sending her even further away from me than she already was physically.

The lift reached the third floor and the soft sound of the automatic opening of the doors brought me back to reality. We walked along the corridor. Irina was in one of the rooms at the end and, as we approached, I felt a trepidation rise up from my legs and spread throughout my body. In a caring voice, Maria asked if everything was OK. I motioned for her to continue. In the meantime, I gasped greedily for breath to quell the agitation, displaying a fake smile of relaxation.

The door to Irina's room was ajar and Maria opened it

slowly. Inside, the nurse was administering medication. Irina was standing with her back towards me, looking out at the grounds. I recognised her thinness and the unmistakable way she wore her hair, tied with a scarf. Although it had been turned grey by the years, the length of her hairstyle was the same as it had been when she was younger. She was wearing black trousers and a turquoise knitted sweater, her favourite colour.

'Morning Maria,' the nurse said. Then, turning to Irina, she added: 'Señora Ester, your daughter has come with a guest.'

Irina didn't answer, nor did she move an inch. Only when she was approached by Maria walking over to greet her did she turn to meet my gaze. A glance consumed in a moment, lost who knows where, swallowed up by the fog of a strange indifference. Then, as if she had seen the nothingness, she looked back at her daughter.

The emotion I felt on seeing the outline of her face was indescribable. Its beauty remained untouched by her advancing years and had remained unchanged over time. It was as if that look, as light as the beating of a butterfly's wings, had generated the power of a hurricane in my heart.

Irina had a bruise on her forehead. A detail that reminded me of her image in one of my nightmares. 'She got it yesterday when she fell over in the garden,' said the nurse, leaving the room. Maria left too. She had clearly sensed my keenness to be alone with Irina. The long journey had come to an end and the much-awaited moment had arrived. With Irina close it seemed as if my life would finally be able to start again.

In that instant a ray of sunshine invaded the room and Irina's face was brightened by a golden light. She let herself be caressed by the glow, remaining seated in the armchair where she had since sat down. I took a few steps forward to get a better look at her, ready to catch her every slight expression. Her gaze appeared sad, directed into the emptiness. In spite of everything, her evasive eyes cast an emerald light. Something told me she had been waiting for me for a long time.

Irina seemed as fragile as a flower that bends and loses its petals in the first gust of wind. I wanted to hold her in a hug, but was too afraid of her unpredictable reaction. I felt hopelessly attracted to her while she, on the contrary, seemed unperturbed and detached from my presence, as if I were a stranger. Irina had completely removed me from what was left of her mind. As aware as I was, I was unable to absorb the pain caused by finding myself confronted by this dramatic reality. I had spent all night preparing for the meeting, but had not expected such indifference. Her striking physical detachment was almost inhuman. I moved closer and recognised the scent of her skin. I felt it penetrate into my nostrils and right up to my brain, intoxicating my sense of smell. I leaned over her to move her hair away from her face. I gently ran a hand over her cheek and whispered: 'Irina, my love, I've come to get you.'

A hint of a smile faded before it hit her lips. Then her expression changed suddenly, giving way to a slight tremor. I noticed her hands stiffen and grab the arms of her chair.

'What are you doing?' she asked, staring at me with the look of a wounded animal. 'Who are you? Where's Fernando? I want Fernando! Please call him. Fernando, Fernando…' she began shouting.

I humoured her, telling her that Fernando would be there soon and she calmed down. I stood up and felt paralysed, in the full grip of an emotional storm. I felt my heart beat in my chest and almost began to weep in despair. I wanted to hug her and take her back in time, to fulfil her dream of living with me. She would once have climbed mountains for it, and had done so! But that memory had vanished, evaporated into the present, which suddenly appeared dark and empty.

'It's me, it's Franco,' I exclaimed.

'Franco?'

'Yes! Do you remember Moscow, the university, the walks along the Moskva?'

A grimace appeared on her face.

'Moscow...' she replied.

'Yes, your city!'

I knelt down and hugged her around her waist, resting my head on her legs. She caressed me instinctively.

'I've never been to Moscow,' she added.

'Irina, please try to remember! Look at this!' I said, showing her the note she had left me that time in the hospital.

She took it and casually read the message with impeccable Russian pronunciation. A glimmer of light opened in my heart and the hazy sky of her confused thoughts seemed clearer for an instant. But it was just an illusion.

'Why have you come here to get me?' she asked in a feeble voice. 'I'm fine here with Fernando.'

'Because I love you, I love you.'

I told her once, twice, a hundred times, without stopping. Then the crying, which I had managed to contain until then, exploded disruptively.

'Come with me!' I shouted, while the tears flooded from my eyes.

'Come with me! Come with me!' I begged.

El Descanso

...

After suffering through that strange meeting with Irina, I left the clinic with a terrible feeling of emptiness. All I had left of her was the weight of despair and a palpable, sharp pain, as if I'd been stabbed. On the way back to San Miguel my thoughts took refuge in a gash in my soul that Irina had unknowingly ripped open with her profound amnesia. I felt a strange sensation of alienation from everything around me and my life seemed to have been turned upside down, as if someone had inadvertently tipped up my hourglass so that I could start all over again, on a different timescale. I had finally found Irina, but I didn't know what to do to repair the damage caused by the terrible disease that had struck her. Before taking me back to the hotel, Maria wanted to stop off at her house.

'I think you should have this,' she said, handing me a wooden box. 'It contains all the things my mother has jealously guarded for a lifetime.'

I thanked her, surprised at first then moved by Maria's unexpected concern. I opened it that evening back at the hotel. It contained two letters tied with a rubber band, newspaper clippings, an old notebook, a gold watch and a brooch. It was the latter that drew my attention. It was the flat, thin butterfly brooch I had given her for her birthday. I had got it on the black market with the help of someone from the party. In exchange, I'd managed, as a foreigner, to procure a number of items for them that were strictly forbidden to Russian citizens.

Irina loved butterflies. She said they had a secret life and were symbols of joy and lightness. I dusted off the memories of when I had given it to her.

That afternoon we met as usual at the Bosco Café. I was sitting at a table with the package in one hand and a rose in the other. I saw her arrive out of breath, went over to meet her and kissed her. She smelled like the rain. As I hugged her the rose fell to the ground and she started laughing. People stopped what they were doing to watch the scene as Irina and I, entwined together, danced happily in yet another genuine moment of love. 'This is for you,' I said, handing her the package. 'You shouldn't have,' she replied, lying shamelessly as she stared at me with her eyes full of emotion. She threw her arms around my neck and stood there, on tiptoe, kissing me on the lips. Repeatedly.

I could still see the joyful image of her face when I instinctively double-checked the contents of the box. I found the note that accompanied the gift among the papers. Written in Russian, it said 'а твоя хрупкая нежная красота, я люблю тебя'.[4]

I held that declaration of love in my hands to absorb every last drop of its essence. Then I remembered the image of Irina sitting in an armchair, unable to stop trembling, and, for a moment, I thought there was no point in continuing to delude myself. Irina was no longer there.

I pulled out the newspaper clippings: they were from articles published in the early 70s, all written by Ester Laine. The first one I came across was from *Mujeres Mexicanas*, a feminist magazine. It was an article about the issue of indigenous women's rights. I read part of it:

Despite the evolution of Mexican society, indigenous women are suffering increasing oppression and inequality. Excluded from education and the right to private property, for these women subordination becomes a characteristic of their ethnicity. An oppression that, in their case, becomes about economics and gender, as well as class.

I finished reading the articles and picked up the notebook. I opened it at random and found myself confronted by the description of the visit Irina had made to my parents after fleeing the Soviet Union. She had tracked them down to ask for information about me, but the meeting had been disappointing. Added to her dejection at not knowing what had happened to me, Irina also had to contend with the hostile attitude of my mother, whom she described in her notes as 'a cultured and stern woman'. Irina spent only two days in Rome. Then, for fear of being tracked down by her father, she flew to Mexico. The departure was heartbreaking for her.

Rome, 30th April 1964

Franco, my love, I'm sad! There are only a few hours left before I have to leave and taking myself away from Rome is a sacrilege. I thought I would find you, but fate had other ideas. I don't know if anyone will even tell you I came looking for you, but know that I'll always hold onto the hope of seeing you again someday. And in that moment, I will welcome you with open arms and a heart that bleeds no more. I love you, Irina.

Imagining the sound of her voice, I fell asleep with the notebook clutched in my hands. I thanked her for having appeased my loneliness.

'Good night, Irina, my soul. Good night to your sad eyes, to your trembling hands. Good night golden butterfly that seeks out the light!'

The next day I went back to the clinic to see her. Her room was empty and I took the opportunity to leave her the brooch. I placed it on the bedside table with a piece of paper on which I'd written my name. With that gesture, I hoped to revive some recollections that her illness had by now buried in oblivion, dragging our shared memories along with it. The nurse told me Irina was in the garden, with the other patients, watching the weekly show.

The amphitheatre was at the end of a long alleyway decorated with flowers and lush bougainvillea that covered the entire pergola. I walked under it, losing myself in the velvety silence of nature, continuing towards the small audience seated on rustic Russian pine benches arranged in a semi-circle in front of the stage. The patients were captivated by the show being performed by three young actors.

Irina was sitting to one side, with both hands clutching the handles of the purse she was holding on her lap. She seemed rejuvenated, with a relaxed expression on her face and her eyes flickering with light. For the occasion, she was wearing a thin white woollen dress set off by a necklace of blue stones. She was so beautiful and elegant that I couldn't resist the temptation to approach. I took a seat next to her and greeted her naturally. She replied politely, without taking her eyes off the show. She occasionally smiled and the smile appeared in the air like the notes of the old music box one of the actors was showing to the enthralled audience: a carousel with horses that galloped to the rhythm of the music.

Irina was happy. As was I, seeing her like that.

'They're going to be free again!' she said, looking at me.

'Who?' I asked.

'The horses. After the show, they'll be running free on the steppe again,' she replied, hinting entirely unconsciously, but instinctively, to the part of the world in which she had been born and spent a peaceful childhood.

Again, I hoped for a glimmer of light, but again Irina didn't recognise me; it didn't worry me unduly. Despite the inexorable progress of the disease, she still managed to experience moments of light-heartedness. If I could have repeated the scene over and over, I would have.

'The theatre sets you free,' I observed.

Irina looked at me out of the corner of one eye.

'How do you know about that? Are you an actor?'

'No, but I would have liked to have been.'

'I was,' she replied, letting out a smile she immediately concealed with her hand. 'I studied the theatre when I was a girl. My mother sent me to take lessons from an elderly lady who had been part of Diaghilev's company. She was called Olga and she lived near a large square.'

A new emotion rose up from my heart. Finally, Irina had remembered something about the past. Her mind had suddenly brought up a clear image of when she was a child. Acting, for her, was a commitment her mother had imposed on her in a suffocating way until she was fifteen. Then a problem with her vocal cords had forced her to stop. She had told me herself about the endless hours of study with Madam Olga, who had turned a section of her house into a school for the children of the party leaders. For a moment I thought her amnesia had dissolved and she had recognised me. But I was forced to change my mind that time as well.

The music from the music box slowed to a halt and the show came to an end. The actors said their farewells to the audience with a bow and disappeared behind the curtain.

'You know, you remind me of someone,' she said as we walked down the pathway. 'What did you say your name was?'

'Franco,' I repeated for the umpteenth time.

Irina's bizarre and unpredictable manner forced me to consider a different kind of approach towards her. My impatient attitude in wanting to obtain at all costs a sign of recognition of our shared experience came up against the consequences of the disease that enforced a present that differed from what I had imagined. There was no use offering Irina the deepest thoughts of love only to demand the impossible of her in exchange. The only thing I could do was stand by her silently, breathe her breath, listen to her heartbeat and see myself reflected in her unpredictability. Tirelessly, like the sea that laps at the coast, I began working on myself to try to understand that the right thing to do was to fully experience my time with her without wondering too much about the future. And so, over the days that followed, a little at a time, I learned to listen to her silences scented with sandalwood oil, to recite the poems she had written and then forgotten, and, above all, to love her in a new reality.

Juanita the Curandera

A month later

I asked Maria if she would make a tart.

The last time I saw Irina she said she wanted one so I decided to surprise her. We ate it on the veranda at tea time. By now I had established a whole new relationship with Irina that allowed me to chip away at the wall of indifference that had existed between us when we first saw each other again. She had renamed me Pedro and her mind could not be changed. On the other hand, she had got used to my presence and stopped asking for Fernando.

I understood that kindness was the only way to contain the mood swings and moments of anxiety that tormented her intermittently. Such as the time she got so upset because the brooch had disappeared from her bedside table drawer. She was stubbornly convinced it had been stolen by Señora Cecilia – the elderly woman with whom she shared a room – and there was no way to make her see reason. The matter dragged on for a few days before the brooch was eventually found and everything was explained. Irina herself had been behind the brooch's disappearance when she put it, unconsciously, in a shoe.

On another occasion, in the middle of a storm, Irina walked out of the clinic in her dressing gown. I was forced to devise an original way to convince her to go back to her room. Attempting to reason with her proved useless. In the end I succeeded by making an effort to fall into step with her world. Irina allowed herself to be taken by the hand only when she truly understood that she could trust me. The point was to look at life and the rain through her eyes and so I did. I accepted the opportunity she offered me and felt the sensation of freedom for the first time in years. I took off my jacket and shirt and stood in the rain in my vest. To get over my initial embarrassment at finding myself half naked in a public place, I started singing and Irina burst out laughing. The patients looked out curiously from the corridor windows. Some even applauded. The nurses tried their best to persuade them to go back to their rooms.

I took Irina by the hand and we walked along the alleyway, soaking wet and with joy in our hearts. When we got back to her room, Irina flopped down on the bed. I went over to her and thanked her for giving me the experience and encouraging me to step outside – even if only for a few minutes – a life that until then I had lived with predictable, ordinary moderation.

The scene reminded me of our last run through a snowy Moscow garden: Irina had called me 'my love' at the top of her voice and then set off running, challenging me to a race that ended near the frozen fountain. I chased after her, trying to tread in her footprints. But she was more agile and faster than me and I had to pursue her for quite a way before I caught her. We ended up on the ground, in each other's arms, on the fresh snow. We were cold and tired, but happy, because in that moment we promised ourselves the future. But there was nothing left of those promises; time had corroded them as rust does iron.

Irina had opened the doors to her illness and was losing any form of control. Even speaking had become superfluous to her. During my visits she communicated almost exclusively with her gaze, doing so by peering at me from the armchair while I read out excerpts from her novels. For her, speaking was only a foothold, a form of refuge; at other times, however, it was a way of picking out phrases from the forgotten boxes of her now tired mind. Like the time when, half asleep, I heard her repeat a phrase from a book by Bertrand Russell. I had brought it with me from Italy and it had miraculously slipped through the customs checks unnoticed. Irina loved the book because she shared the English philosopher's ideas on how to achieve happiness. She quoted a few sentences from memory with confidence, as if she were reading them right there and then.

I kept remembering the day of the storm. Maria had come to her mother's room with the doctor on duty, who wasted no time reminding us of the clinic's code of conduct. The message was clearly directed to me that, instead of containing a sick woman's extravagant request, I had gone out of my way to encourage her. Maria wasted no time doubling the dose and scolded her mother. Despite her strict tone and wide eyes, the expression on her face betrayed a certain satisfaction at our childish behaviour.

'You really do make a lovely couple,' she said.

Irina failed to react; I stumbled over an explanation.

'She'd gone down into the garden and...'

'And what did you think you were doing?' she interrupted.

'What any man in love would have done for his woman' I replied. 'I tried to convince her, but then I thought the right thing to do was to comply with her request to go for a walk in the rain so I gave in.'

Maria shook her head.

'Do you really think you acted in her best interests? You are aware of my mother's condition, aren't you?'

'I only gave her what she wanted. When we were young, back in Moscow, we would do it all the time. Your mother used to love running through the snow.'

Tears came to Maria's eyes and she pretended to be arranging something in the wardrobe to hide her embarrassment. But it didn't take long before she returned to the argument.

'How did you get her back inside?'

'I promised her we would do it again.'

'OK... OK... Do whatever you like!' she said, bringing an end to the discussion.

After that episode, my relationship with Maria became friendlier and more relaxed. In the evening, on my way back from the clinic, I would sometimes have dinner with her and her children and it gave me the chance to get to know her better. Once I even asked her to tell me about her father. 'I don't remember him at all. I was two when he died in the accident. If you want to know anything else, you just have to read what the newspapers said about him to get an idea.'

'Did your mother love him?'

Maria answered with a shrug.

'What do you want me to say? She only ever talked about him on rare occasions, as if she'd deliberately erased him from her past. Despite knowing that a life without love is not a life, my mother decided to tie herself to the first person who asked her to marry him. She did it to try to forget you,' she added, looking me in the eyes.

'She's always been what I wanted too,' I replied.

'That's not the point,' she hastened to add. 'After her failed attempt to track you down at your parents' house, my mother carried on loving you as if you were imaginary. In the pain of not knowing what had happened to you, she chose instead to live in a marriage that only appeared to make her happy. But there's no doubt that my father's world represented something new to her, a false paradise into which she, too naïvely, plunged headlong.'

Maria made observations about her mother's marriage while I tried to imagine what Irina was like in those years, what kind of a life she had led and what had driven her to take such an important step. Like me, she had been unlucky not to have found a way to turn her dreams into reality. But perhaps some of the responsibility also fell at our feet. We should have got to know ourselves first in order to get closer to what we wanted. Her marriage and my change of identity represented two sides of the same coin: failure, something we were finally breaking down.

Maria was increasingly coming round to the idea of seeing me by her mother's side and I confessed my real intentions to her: to take Irina back to Paris with me to live the rest of our lives together. It was a plan that had slipped into uncertainty due to her illness, but I had yet to give up on it completely.

The meeting I had with a very special person a few days later would prove to be providential in finding a way out of this apparent dead-end situation.

Maria had already beeped her horn a couple of times to let me know she was waiting outside. She had come to pick me up at the Puertecita to take me to the clinic as she did every morning. I looked at my watch and realised I was later than usual. I washed quickly, finished getting dressed and left the bathroom.

A stinging pain stabbed my temples and I almost passed out. Instinctively I closed my eyes and, when I opened them again, I saw a series of floating black dots. I lost my balance and fell over. I felt my body let go, ran a hand over my mouth and realised my nose was bleeding. The haemorrhage lasted a few minutes; the liquid streamed out, soaking my beard and dripping down my neck. I could feel its metallic taste in my throat. I had to tilt my head to one side and cough several times to stop from choking. I shouted for help but couldn't make myself heard. Then I tried to pull myself up, clinging to the arm of the chair. But even that attempt failed and I collapsed back onto the ground, abandoned to my fate while Maria, unaware, beeped her horn yet again to get me to hurry up.

Shortly afterwards, she appeared, somewhat concerned, with the owner of the hotel. They both lifted me up and laid me on the bed; Maria made me drink a glass of water and sugar while the hotel owner kept my legs raised. I slowly began to get my strength back and the problem with my eyes subsided.

'Don't worry Señor Franco,' said the hotel owner. 'It's probably because of the altitude. It can take a long time to get used to, you know?'

'Maybe,' I replied. 'Although I've never had any issues with my blood pressure before.'

Something suddenly came to Maria and she went into

the other room and made a phone call. She came back a little later, visibly relieved.

'I know who you should see if you want to find out why you collapsed,' she said.

The hotel owner understood who Maria was referring to. An unequivocal understanding flashed between the pair. I got up from the bed and felt the blood start flowing normally in my veins again; my breathing and heartbeat had also returned to their regular rhythms. Maria had been very frightened to see me like that and she wasted no time making me an appointment. In truth, I was also shocked by what had happened and, as we were leaving the hotel, I asked if there was a pharmacy where I could have my blood pressure checked.

'Are you taking me to a doctor?' I asked.

'Not exactly,' she replied. 'I'm trying to help you. You just have to trust me.'

Maria spoke with the kindness of a daughter and a smile she had never given me before. Her affectionate manner prodded at my emotions and I made up my mind to follow her. In return, I asked her only to remove the distance between us and call me Franco.

'OK, Franco. Let's go, or we'll be late,' she said, hugging me.

We drove towards San Marcos de Begoña, a town a quarter of an hour from San Miguel.

'Can you tell me where you're taking me?'

'Wait and see.'

'I feel better now. I don't need to see anyone. Irina's waiting for me.'

'Don't worry, Franco. I've already told the clinic you won't be going until this afternoon.'

'OK, but where are we going?' I asked again.

'I want you to meet someone. Her name is Juanita and she's a very famous *curandera*. She'll be able to tell you what happened to you.'

'Are you talking about a healer?'

'Call it what you want. She's a woman with many skills and an inner strength she uses to help others. Juanita has managed to win the trust of the people around here because she's often shown that she knows how to look deep inside people.'

On the way, Maria talked about Juanita with a profound respect, stressing several times the importance of the meeting I was about to have. She said I was lucky, that Juanita was so popular, she wasn't always able to see everyone. It all seemed absurd to me. If I'd had a choice, I would have gone straight to see Irina. Nonetheless, in order to satisfy Maria's insistence, I went along with her decision.

We arrived in San Marcos and took a dirt track that ended near Ignacio Allende Lake. We parked in front of a very modest house, with stone walls and a wooden roof. As soon as we got out of the car, a woman about fifty, of medium height, with raven hair and copper-coloured skin, came to meet us.

'This way,' she said, gesturing to us.

'That's her daughter,' Maria whispered. 'She helps her.'

We walked into the courtyard of the house to join three other people waiting to be received by the *curandera*. They were seated on straw chairs arranged in the shade of a giant white cedar. The first in line was a middle-aged man, a *campesino*, who hid a profound mystery in his dark eyes. His face was parched from the sun and his hands thickened with calluses that could only have been caused by years of hard work with a spade. He wore an iron crucifix around his neck. Every now and then he would grab it with both hands, bring it up to his mouth and kiss it in thanks. He repeated the gesture like a ritual, whispering words in a language that Maria explained to me was the ancient Aztec language Nahuatl.

Two women were sitting next to him: mother and daughter. The young woman was a stunning Native American girl with a slender physique and soft, elegant facial features like those of a cat. She was curiously watching a pair of parrots inside a cage tied to a tree branch. Her mother occupied her time as she waited by knitting a woollen hat, the clicking needles keeping up a constant rhythm.

'She suffers from nervous disorders,' she explained to Maria and me to justify their presence. 'She has bad dreams at night,' she added. Then, going over to her daughter, she said in a whisper: 'Juanita's good, you'll see.'

The girl lowered her eyes to escape her mother's intrusive chatter.

'And why are you here?' asked the woman, taking a break from her knitting but not from the desire for conversation.

I wasn't in the mood for talking and, pretending to be interested in a book I'd glimpsed on a table near the front door, I got up and walked across the courtyard. Alongside a volume entitled *The Power of Herbal Healers* were two framed photographs, the statuette of an angel, some dried leaves and a copper jar full of candles, amulets, stones and other objects. On the ground, in a corner, I noticed a camping stove, kept alight with a soft flame. It held an earthenware pot that was giving off puffs of steam. Overwhelmed by curiosity, I removed the lid and was hit by the aromatic scent of alfalfa.

I suddenly felt as if I was on the set of an Almodóvar film, surrounded by larger-than-life characters with whom I was sharing a surreal experience. Maria continued to hold firm in her decision to arrange the meeting for me and, from time to time, threw me reassuring glances. I had almost dozed off when the door opened and the *curandera* finally came out.

'It's her!' said Maria, enthusiastically.

Juanita was an elderly woman with generous eyes and a sincere smile. Behind her, a young woman with a baby in her arms was thanking her repeatedly, crying with joy. The *curandera* took a bag of herbs from a trunk and handed it to her: 'Drink the infusion every night before you go to sleep and take care of yourself.' She then kissed the baby's head and sent the woman away.

Despite being sceptical about forms of healing not recognised by traditional medicine, the image of that happy mother moved me deeply. Her eyes sparkled with gratitude and, although I didn't know the reason for her visit, it was clear that Juanita had been able to provide her with answers to the questions that were troubling her. Maybe the solution to her problem was just an illusion, but at that moment it seemed right to think of letting her believe it. Although I continued to doubt the power of shamans, especially when it came to healing physical ailments, I became convinced of what Maria had told me about the power of the *curandera*: by tapping into the arcane energies of the spirit, Juanita could instil hope in patients, just as she had done for that young mother.

Juanita's daughter motioned for the *campesino* to enter the house and the *curandera* began her consultation. We had to wait two hours before it was my turn. Juanita greeted me with a smile in a dimly lit room, full of candles and sacred images. Without even asking me why I was there, she made me take my shirt off and began rubbing me with a bundle of pirul grass. I felt her drag the leaves across my body, dry at first then moistened with a solution that smelled of cedar and tobacco. After the ritual, which I only later realised served to purify the spirit, Juanita handed the bunch of grass to her daughter who, after sprinkling it abundantly with alcohol, set fire to it on the brazier. Only then was I told to lie down on a day bed and keep my eyes closed while the *curandera* began reciting the Lord's Prayer.

She finished praying and fell silent once more. I could feel her standing next to me with her hands on her chest. I was about to tell her what had happened to me when she said, as if she had read my mind: 'I will treat your spirit as a life force without affecting the symptoms of your body. Whatever the illness was, the cause was spiritual and the ailment you experienced comes from an imbalance. I will cure your imbalance.'

The woman's statement seemed strange. Then, shortly afterwards, something happened that would help me understand the meaning of what she had just said. Meanwhile, Juanita's fingertips moved over my body, grazing my skin. I could feel them pause delicately and give off a kind of warmth. With precise, slow movements, she traced imaginary anticlockwise circles, exploring each limb a little at a time. When she started stroking the veins in my wrist, I felt my nose bleed again. I opened my eyes with a start and she gently ran a hand over my eyelids to close them.

'Love has a direct relationship to the heart,' she said in a soft voice, 'and the power to love is within us, like fear. It's up to us to choose to open the doors of our hearts.'

She dabbed my blood with a perfumed handkerchief and

continued drawing circles. Juanita sensed my agitation and reassured me: 'Don't worry, it's your energy moving around.'

A few minutes passed, then Juanita's daughter approached and the ritual came to an end. Together they lifted me up to a sitting position: 'Now, drink this in one go,' said one of the two women. I swallowed a hot, oily, sweet-tasting liquid and in no time at all a soporific power enveloped my mind. The effect was amazing: an unstoppable force threw me back into the past to retrace my entire existence with lightning-fast re-enactments. A perception that went beyond human limits and penetrated into a limbo that only the subconscious can access. It was like running along an impervious path, pursued by myself and glimpsing scenes of moments lived with Irina, my mother, my party comrades, Giovanni and the students in Paris. A breathless reconstruction of my life that ended in the sea, flying off a cliff, dazzled by the sun, as bright as the light that welcomes us before dying… or being reborn. Dazed by the leap into the sea, I let myself be lulled by the waves like a shipwreck set adrift. Meanwhile, I listened to Juanita's muffled voice before falling into a deep numbness.

'Now you have more energy and can find your guide. Try to relive the memory, paying attention to the signs that appear suddenly and allow yourself to be carried away by the flow.'

When I woke up, I was in another room and Maria was sitting near the bed. I was completely bathed in sweat and I felt as if something inside me was starting to change. Juanita's advice, dictated in the midst of an inner journey, had clearly not been ignored, but assimilated by my subconscious.

'How do you feel?' Maria asked, taking my hand.

'How long was I asleep?' I answered.

'Six, seven hours. I don't know. I lost count.'
'An eternity!'
'Yes. You talked a lot as well.'
'What did I say?'
'Incomprehensible words to start with. Then you mentioned my mother a lot.'

I stood up, staggering. Maria moved quickly to support my arm.

'Can we go now?'
'Yes. Juanita is waiting for you.'

The *curandera* was out on the road, looking at the sun on the horizon. Half of the sky had turned red and the clouds looked as if they were fraying over the mountains. Everything seemed huge, eternal. After Maria reassured me that she had convinced the *curandera* to accept a donation, I approached to say my goodbyes: Juanita had warm hands and a reassuring look. I was gripped by an undeniable instinct to embrace her. She reciprocated.

'The power to choose is within you.'

I didn't answer. I broke away from the long embrace, got into the car with Maria and we left slowly, leaving behind a trail of dust and mystery. I turned to look at her one last time and saw her in the middle of the road, in conscious solitude, looking at the sun on the horizon.

...

The visit to the *curandera* gave me no respite, as I might have imagined. The 'power to choose' that she had mentioned when we said goodbye referred to the decision I had to make with Irina. Although she had not explicitly said so, my sudden illness was linked to the same problem.

From the day of the meeting, I spent a week reconsidering

my thoughts. Except for a few brief visits to Irina, I spent hours and hours shut in my hotel room mulling over what to do. I felt that the time to leave was approaching; all I had to do was set the day.

One afternoon I called Faustine to tell her I was in Mexico and would be coming home soon. She asked if I had finally found Irina; I said yes and she let out a cry of joy. But then she sensed a certain uneasiness in the tone of my voice and my vague response. I didn't feel like telling her the state I had found Irina in and I wasn't particularly enthusiastic about the conversation. Faustine changed the subject, reminding me to let her know the date I would be coming back; she would pick me up at the airport.

Not knowing how to make my decision, one night I drowned my thoughts in alcohol. I got myself a bottle of whiskey, which kept me company all night, sitting on the hotel terrace. I emptied the glass into my stomach twice in a row and lit a cigarette. The alcohol began to hammer in my brain and a feeling of abandonment came over my legs.

The cool north wind blew intermittently like the breath of a giant beyond the mountain. It seeped into my room, blowing the curtain. The shadows, as restless as my mood, drew abstract shapes on the wall. I smoked and wondered what to do. I even asked the moon for advice. I gripped the bottle and drank some more. Then I closed my eyes and imagined walking along the Seine with Irina. I began to smile.

Irina had never been to Paris: I had told her about the history of the city, described its monuments and invited her to the Bistrot de l'Absinthe. I would take every possible precaution to look after Irina: I would call on my doctor friend and ask my neighbour for advice. Faustine would give me a hand, caring for her lovingly. I would prepare everything, down to the smallest detail. But what if that wasn't the right solution for her? I wondered. What if my thinking was pervaded with a deep sense of selfishness? I became realistic again and concluded that some diseases impose drastic solutions. Irina needed such a decision.

It was four in the morning. Absolute silence reigned once more in the alleyways of San Miguel, even the last restaurant had switched off its lights. I thought about Irina again and began crying as I staggered towards the bed. The next morning, I woke up with the sun on my face and hurting all over. I tried to move to find out where I was and my hand struck the bottle, which fell to the floor. The same fate befell the ashtray, which ended up upside down on the ground.

With difficulty I got up, or at least tried to, while a sense of nausea upset my stomach. I could barely stand and stumbled several times to get to the bathroom, where I crawled into the shower, which turned out to be very refreshing. After a gruelling night, I had made up my mind: the next step was to talk to Irina.

I called for a taxi and went to the clinic. It was a delicate moment and, before meeting Irina, I had to search inside myself for the right words so as not to upset her already precarious balance. I had been seeing her regularly for about forty days now, a long enough period for a person who, due to their illness, lived almost entirely in the present.

For her I was always Pedro and I'd become part of her daily life thanks to the unusual attachment she had developed towards me. She would continuously ask the doctors about me whenever they checked in on her and, when they discharged Señora Cecilia from the clinic, she even asked

Maria to let me spend the night with her. I had accepted her extravagant way of loving me. I felt her affection. Several times she curled up in my arms, letting herself be lulled by the unconditional love I felt for her.

On the way to the clinic, I saw a girl holding a basket, selling bunches of flowers by the side of the road. I asked the taxi driver to pull over and bought one. The flowers were strelitzias. The scent began to spread through the car like a cloud.

'Great choice!' said the taxi driver. 'Around here we call them birds of paradise. They represent elegance.'

Elegance, I thought, like Irina's beauty. I paused to gaze at the flowers with large orange petals and suddenly the noise of the wheels on the gravel car park woke me from the spell.

I went to Irina's room and found her reading, oddly.

'Pedro!' she exclaimed.

I looked at her with love.

'Did you bring flowers?'

'Yes, they're for you,' I answered, gently offering her a kiss on the cheek.

I gave them to her and she inhaled their wonderful scent. She stared at them for a moment. She had a dazed expression, like Sleeping Beauty in the fairy-tale.

'They're scented,' she said, stroking one.

I put the flowers in a vase and placed it on the bedside table.

I tried to start the speech I had prepared, but the words came out of my mouth in a jumble, like when I was a child and I'd forgotten the poem I was supposed to have learned by heart. I started over, making up a story, as if I was referring to someone else, but I ran out of steam that time too. The room quickly filled with silence. I spent the whole afternoon sitting opposite Irina without managing to utter a word or, at least, none of those I had intended to tell her.

In my heart I knew this was our last meeting, that all the love I had recovered, rekindled and nurtured throughout my long journey would remain a soft, sweet and ethereal memory, to be added, like a vivid link, to the poignant chain that bound me to Irina. The future she had left to live would not be peaceful and taking her with me to Paris would only have served to satisfy my own self-love. The right to love her, as I had claimed and been able to externalise, had to come to terms with her stay in the country to which she had committed herself for fifty years through her writing, politics and love for a daughter.

Maria would accompany her to the end. It was right for me to step aside. After all, I had reappeared in her life out of nowhere and slipped into her mind, between the small spaces that the disease had left free, for a little while longer. I had decided to walk away from her, listening to the power of my feelings for her, as the *curandera* had suggested. To uproot Irina from the country she had nourished and that had nourished her spirit in return would have been nothing but forced. And so, paradoxically, that evening spent with her was my last act of love.

'Take care of yourself,' I said, after kissing her at length on the lips.

Irina put a finger to my mouth as if to silence me. A dark veil covered the light in her eyes and she faded suddenly like the flame of a consumed candle.

A tear ran down her face.

Going Home

When I saw Maria that evening, I could still feel the loss that my meeting with her mother had provoked in me. The weight of that tear was imprinted on my heart like an open wound. I hadn't felt such a great, intense, all-consuming pain in years.

The memory of Irina's farewell was merciless, like that of the last kiss I had given her. But an inner voice told me I had done the right thing. Mine had been a necessary, unavoidable choice and perhaps that sudden departure was the price I had to pay for transforming the natural desire to want to see her again after so many years into an obsessive form of possession that had gone beyond every limit, even that of her illness.

The following morning, I would leave for Mexico City and from there board the first flight to Paris. When I told Maria everything, she understood my decision completely.

'I felt it,' she explained, looking at me with admiration. 'I would never have asked you because the decision had to be yours, but I believe it's the right choice. My mother is getting worse by the day and she wouldn't have been able to cope.'

Maria's words exuded objectivity and a good dose of

balance, but her voice did not. She was sad to know that I was leaving. The love story between her mother and I had touched her. She had got used to my presence and it was clear that she had grown fond of me. Speculation about my future in Paris was the only topic of conversation that evening. Maria wanted to know how I would deal with the loneliness once I got home. I explained that, thanks to my experience with her mother, I had learned to live in the present and only there. I would carry on like that, day after day, letting the future forget about me and I about it.

When the moment came to say goodbye, I tried to downplay it:

'I'm leaving you my Irina,' I said with a smile. 'Take care of her.'

I walked away.

Maria remained motionless for a moment. Then she ran down the stairs towards me and gave me another hug.

'Thank you for what you've done,' she said softly. 'Keep in touch.'

Melancholy flooded into my veins and clouded my eyes. I could no longer conceal the discomfort I was feeling. I cleared my throat to cover the embarrassment and tried to say something useful to muffle the sad atmosphere that had sprung up between us. The result was the same. Maria went back into the house, pulling the door closed behind her and not looking back. With that scene I had ended another chapter of my fairy-tale with Irina.

Back at the hotel, I stopped to look at the church of San Miguel for the last time. At that time in the evening, it was lit by a bright moon. I said goodbye to the narrow streets of the centre, the small colonial town's colourful houses and its irrevocable silence.

4th October

My thoughts about Irina wandered to a remote place while I was in the air. It was about an hour into the flight and I was looking out of the window, as if she might appear at any moment alongside the clouds floating in the sky. I imagined her lit by the sun, lying on a carpet of white clouds as she called me by my real name. I knew I was daydreaming, as I already had been several times during the trip, but if Irina really had appeared, I would have returned her image to the wind to set her free, keeping the promise I had made to her.

I wondered how she was reacting to my absence. It was the three days since we had seen each other. Part of me hoped the disease would take care of it and make her forget everything, so that she could continue to live as before. On the other hand, I dreamt that the gentle memory of an extraordinary experience would stay with her. Irina and I had rekindled the feeling that time and distance had stifled and exchanged something different, delicate and penetrating, like light rain filtering through the thick foliage of a tree.

I was on my way home. I was exhausted, but at the same time content with the opportunity I had given myself. 'It's a pity Giovanni isn't with us anymore,' I thought, struggling to come to terms with the reality that was so bitter for me. I would have told him everything in detail. He would have understood the reason for my metamorphosis and appreciated the effort I had made.

My metamorphosis, that really was it.

The journey I was about to conclude had brought about a profound change, both on a personal level and in the reality in which I lived. My identity had been changed, not by a divine being, wizard or witch, but by the internal and ongoing transformation I had subjected myself to, without realising it, the moment I decided to set off in search of Irina. A journey designed to bring about an inevitable change, a consequence of a sort of personal 'panta rhei'.

Something important inside me had changed, above all the way I looked at the things in life I had systematically avoided before. Finding Irina had not been easy, least of all the decision to tear myself away from her. Yet, in that horribly real experience, in which I had transformed myself from an adventurer driven mad by love into someone capable of healing myself, I had found the light. Seen from the outside, my behaviour might have appeared inconsistent and contradictory; someone else in my place might not have given up on living out his final years with the woman he loved. I, on the other hand, while acting with love, had chosen to do the opposite. The fact is that some inner voices cannot be ignored; they appear as warning messages, showing you the way. Something similar had also happened to me in Russia: the people I had met and the places I had visited were linked to each other and to a very particular meaning that I had to grasp in order to understand who I really was.

In my hand luggage, along with Irina's notebook, I had the two letters I had found in her wooden box. I only had to glance at them to recognise her handwriting. They were both missing the addressee. I read part of one of them.

I will never stop thanking you. Without your help I would never have won my freedom. The organisation was perfect and even here, the final destination on my journey, I found people who were kind and willing to help me. All thanks to you! For now, I'm working in a factory, but I'm thinking about leaving and enrolling at university.

Unfortunately, I haven't seen Franco again. No one knows anything about him. It's as if he's disappeared into thin air. Believe me, I've tried everything to track him down, but it's been useless.

Although the name of the person who should have read those words was missing, it was clear that Irina was talking to Igor. The fact that those letters were still in the box reminded me of Igor's suppositions about the cautious approach Irina would have forced herself to adopt once she arrived in Mexico.

After reading the letters, I went back to browsing through the pages of the notebook. Leafing through them, I found Irina's account of the Tlatelolco Massacre, one of the darkest moments in Mexico's recent history, in which she too, along with thousands of demonstrators, had played a part. The autobiographical tale was entitled *Tlatelolco: the perfect trap* and was part of her novel *No Doubt*, published in 1990. I read it in one go.

I stumbled in the stampede, hitting my right knee hard on the stairs. A faculty colleague came to my rescue: 'Come on, Ester. We need to get away!' he said, holding out his hand. He didn't have the time to pull me up. A stray shot pierced his head and he fell, dead, a few inches from me. I stayed down. I couldn't believe my eyes as I saw the patch of red blood spread slowly over the white marble steps. Someone panicked, stepping on me to save themselves. Isabel, my friend, had a swollen face and a nasty wound on her neck. My other comrades from the 'brigada' were all missing. Gunshots and bursts of machine-gun fire echoed around the building, which, in the space of just a few minutes, had become a trap. The student leaders had sought shelter on the third floor. Some tried to climb down from the balcony, but armed plain-clothes soldiers broke in and captured almost all of them. I dragged myself down the flight of stairs, crawling on the ground in pain, and reached the second floor. I tried to get up, but couldn't and collapsed against the wall. Isabel was crying and trembling like a leaf. There was general bewilderment around us; people were running away screaming under an incessant hail of bullets. Amid the chaos, the sound of a walkie-talkie caught my attention. I turned and saw a man talking into it agitatedly. He was trying to establish radio contact: 'Olympia Battalion, Olympia Battalion, come in Olympia Battalion.'

He was with a guy who was waving his gun in the air and giving orders to round up the other members of the battalion.

'Is everyone here? Where are the others?' he shouted.

My gaze met Isabel's and we understood: they were snipers. They too, like those we had seen on the third floor, were wearing civilian clothes and white gloves on their left hands. Across the corridor, we noticed a man with the same sign of recognition who, positioned at the window, was firing repeatedly on the crowd. The soldiers were responding to the attack, as someone was trying to direct operations. The voice came from outside: 'Don't shoot. They're wearing white gloves. Don't shoot!'

Isabel and I steeled ourselves and went down to the ground floor. The military were arresting every student they came across in the building, forcing them to stand against the wall, with their hands behind their necks and their trousers removed. Most of them showed signs of having been beaten. Meanwhile, all hell was breaking loose outside. The signal to attack the protesters in the square had been given by a green flare that had ripped across the sky, cutting through the air from the old church of Santiago Tlatelolco to the Chihuahua Building. From the helicopter, a machine gun opened fire on the unarmed demonstrators below, while the soldiers advanced in large numbers from the Aztec ruins and the right-hand side of the church. Within a few minutes they blocked all the exits from the square, forcing the demonstrators to flee in the same direction, packed together like rats, while members of the Olimpia Battalion continued shooting like crazy from the floors of the Chihuahua Building.

The screams, crying and fear of the fleeing students, many of them wounded and terrified, echoed around the square, marking the saddest day of the Mexican student movement with despair and blood. That evening, the dead and wounded gathered as darkness fell. The imprint of the pain and suffering of those corpses was still there, perceptible in the air and on the paving of that large square.

Irina's account, enhanced by the touching testimonies of other students, continued with some reflections on the movement.

In '68, those of us who were students at the UNAM,[5] profoundly influenced by what had happened in Paris in May and our colleagues at the American universities of Berkeley and Columbia, came together and made our voices heard. I was in my final year of political science. I was a CNH delegate and part of the 'Brigada Verdad,' which aimed to provide counter-information to El Sol and other newspapers aligned with the Diaz Ordaz government. At that time, the university was experiencing a great political and cultural ferment. There was an inscription on the entrance door to the faculty that summarised how things were back then: 'Civic conscience has woken up and the Mexican family has become politicised.'

We wanted to shout to the world that we were united and ready to fight. People trusted us and listened to us. As well as those of us who were students, there were professors, intellectuals and workers in the movement. There were countless initiatives, almost always supported by large swathes of the population. Some of our protests were noticed more than others for their originality. Like, on 13th September, the silent demonstration we organised to demonstrate to the community that our silence was more eloquent than words, which had been violated and, in many cases, extinguished by the soldiers' bayonets. That time we left the Museum of Anthropology to go to the Plaza de la Costitución, where a big meeting was planned. For the entire duration of the march we stayed gagged as a sign of protest. Two hundred thousand of us covered our mouths with handkerchiefs and adhesive tape, marching in silence, waging a civic battle that has gone down in history.

During that demonstration, only our footsteps could be heard and the silence rang out for all Mexicans, much louder than the government's repression.

I paused to imagine that silent mass, taking to the streets of Mexico City to show that the students were neither vandals nor 'rebels without a cause', as they had often been labelled. I turned the page and finished reading the description of that fateful day of 2nd October.

My name had been included in the schedule of speakers, before Garín. It was not the first time I'd spoken in public. I would often give speeches at gatherings or chant slogans during demonstrations, but the idea of doing it from the third floor of the Chihuahua Building in front of a square full of people made me uneasy. To prepare, I'd asked Isabel to come with me to the rally early in the afternoon and wait there for the rest of our comrades. Light rain fell from the leaden sky as more and more people slowly arrived in the square. As well as the huge student presence, there were also delegations of workers who arrived proudly showing off their banners. A lengthy applause greeted the union of railway workers when they entered the square; they had always been closest to our struggle. Ordinary people had also responded to the call to demonstrate: couples with children, elderly people, who approached curiously, and, inevitably, street vendors. As well as claiming greater freedom, the reason for the rally was to announce to the people a hunger strike in support of the political prisoners, including the last students and teachers who had been arrested during the demonstrations of 18th and 23rd September. The strike would last for ten days and its end would coincide with the start of the Olympics. The city centre was closed to traffic and the only way to get to the square was on foot. I wandered through the crowd with a strange presentiment. The huge numbers of police officers at every access route did not bode well. What Ordaz had said a month earlier about the riots in the city caused by our demonstrations suddenly rang out like a threat.

'We will do whatever we have to do!' he said, speaking to the nation.

And so they did: to preserve order and prove they were capable of hosting an international event like the Olympics, they perpetrated a massacre.

Irina's words breached my understanding of political commitment in general. Unlike me, who had experienced activism as a boy and then transformed it into something more personal through teaching, Irina had made it a reason for living, choosing the path of continuous and constant militancy since her university days in 1968.

Discovering that Irina had personally experienced the massacre in the Plaza de la Tres Culturas also made me reflect on another aspect: the *desaparición* in Mexico. The truth about the number of dead, wounded, arrested and missing after the massacre was never ascertained. What is not in doubt is that students in Mexico have always been victims of bloody acts of violence. I closed the notebook and was reminded of the most recent story of the forty-three students who had disappeared from the city of Iguala on 26th September last year.

And Now... the Present

Paris, 5th October

I'm disorientated.

I could lose myself in this silence.

Faustine has just left and here I am, alone, looking out over the rooftops of Paris from my apartment terrace once more. It's evening and the stars have just begun to shine, unperturbed by the huge clouds appearing on the horizon. I move from room to room carefully examining the furniture, paintings and objects in this house that now seem cold and bare to me. I do it as a mental exercise, to extrapolate from my memory any elements that might make me relocate myself, as quickly and as painlessly as possible, in the present. Seventy-one days away from home are by no means few, especially if they are spent chasing a woman across the world.

I finish my brief reconnaissance and go back to my usual rituals: I light a Gauloise, fill a glass with Martell, my favourite cognac, and sit down in a living room armchair. 'Welcome back!' I repeat to myself, pretending to feel comfortable. Perhaps I should have made Faustine stay a little longer; at least then I wouldn't have suffered this terrible loneliness.

As promised, Faustine came to pick me up at the airport. On the way home, she asked about Irina and I told her everything in great detail. She listened without asking too many questions; she must have understood that there are some love stories nourished more by distance and memories, not needing words to be relived. Perhaps she was expecting a happy ending to the story, like a Hollywood film, but happiness doesn't always prevail in real life. There are people in love who never manage to meet, to overcome the absence that divides them, choosing to live in solitude. 'That's love too,' I explained to her.

When it comes to couples, union does not mean a perfect fit, or at least it may not be a necessary condition. Feeling destined for someone, however, can imply a continuous wait, which may turn out to be longer than life itself. Waiting and loving can be the same thing.

Nevertheless, I realise that starting again isn't easy. The silence insinuates itself everywhere, causing my soul to waver for a moment. The images of my trip seem to belong to a distant time, but the taste of Irina's kiss has stayed on my lips. That contact, that final contact, lasted an eternity. Impossible to forget.

I'm not tired and I have nothing to do, other than to try to sum up the balance of life yet again. I decide to try now, fresh from emotions and memories. It feels as if it will be a long night.

Like a reporter scrupulously enunciating events that have been observed and explored, I begin to focus on the moments spent between Paris and San Miguel. I catalogue them one by one and clarify their meaning, trying to extract the truth from each of them. It's not an easy task, I know. I don't concern myself with the appropriateness of the choices

I made, but with the distinction between true and false in every action, word and idea. In addition to what I always told Giovanni, the search for truth has been an obsession that has haunted me for years, but which I'm now finally ready to face.

I start with identity. The journey has allowed me to completely strip myself of the name Enrico Ceccarelli in a natural way, free from trauma. It was as if I had suddenly taken off an ill-fitting garment to relieve myself of the weight of the sad framework that I had constructed to erase the difficult memories of the past and guarantee myself a peaceful life. I got my real name back thanks to an inner metamorphosis that symbolically allowed me to celebrate a true rebirth. It was like re-immersing myself in the amniotic fluid of genesis and leaving the womb of life as a new individual. To go beyond the fine line of recognition I had to rebuild myself, through meeting people who were completely unaware of the false balance I had created. From that moment on, the name Enrico Ceccarelli began to sound surprisingly foreign and cumbersome to me. Now that I was home again, it even seemed odd to read it above my doorbell. I no longer needed a double identity and running away didn't make sense anymore. My old name has vanished, dissolved into thin air, leaving room for the real one.

The transformation had also infected my thoughts about politics and changed some of the considerations about ideology I had directed towards myself over those long years. I had acknowledged my dissent against the theories I had believed in from an early age. An awareness that I gained after personally experiencing the consequences of the mystification of the truth perpetuated by a regime that succeeded in imposing power for years. Despite the disillusionment and everything it generated in my personal understanding of politics, I wasn't angry at absolute communism; in the past, I had exposed myself to other political beliefs with the same determination. The critical mediation of the Soviet doctrine was dictated by an independence that has always marked my character and an incurable curiosity for the things that surround me. Beyond colours and various flags, I firmly condemn everything that binds political action to ferocity, cruelty and revenge, and I rarely agree with those who believe the end justifies the means in politics.

The journey also showed me the different political path taken by Irina. The experience of '68, seen from the perspective of the Mexican students, allowed her to bring out her genuine vocation for social commitment. And while I, having found myself in difficulty at the university in Moscow, could not help but make a definitive break with ideology, she managed to claim the principle of freedom as an inalienable right. Mexico, for Irina, represented the 'realm of necessity' to which she dedicated all her physical commitment and mental energy.

I looked at the clock hanging on the wall. It was just before eleven. My stomach must have noticed too as I heard it rumble. I went into the kitchen and made myself something to eat. So that I wouldn't feel alone, I set the table for two, arranging the plates and cutlery carefully in the middle of the table before lighting a coloured candle. Like a chess player who acts out their opponent's moves, I move from one chair to the other to begin a rather ridiculous scene. I go on like this for a while, then turn on the stereo and put on some music. I pour the wine into the glasses and gently bring them together, simulating a toast with Irina: 'We are united by a thread. You will always be with me!' I tell her. I take a sip from both glasses and the magic begins.

I'm struck by how I feel. I talk to Irina as if I had sat down next to her to warm my soul and, at times, I even hear her voice. We go on like this for the whole dinner and slowly the wound caused by the distance closes. Irina is inside me and this is enough to feel good, even if I'm aware I will never see her again. Nobody can understand, but soon the memory of her will no longer hurt so much. I feel as if I love her more than before and this will save me.

The unexpected ringing of the telephone distracts me from my thoughts. I pick it up and hear Faustine's voice: 'Professore, I'm sorry it's so late, but I was wondering if you needed anything?'

I appreciate the thought and thank her, as I take the novel by Irina that El Gordo gave me out of my suitcase.

'I'm not tired, so I think I'll do some reading,' I reply.

We exchange a few more sentences before I end the conversation. I sit down in an armchair with the intention of immersing myself in one of the famous Ester Montoya's stories.

I open the book with a certain curiosity and notice something fall out onto the carpet.

I look down instinctively to see what it is and smile.

I pick up Irina's butterfly brooch and hold it tightly in one hand as I begin to read.

Rome 22nd January 2016

Dear Professor Franco Solfi,
  A month has passed since we met in the Galleria Esedra bar in Rome and it has not been a single day that I have not thought about your story.
  I have let it take hold of me to the extent that I can identify with a reality that, even if I can only imagine it, has moved me, made me dream and, most importantly, made me reflect.
  It is as if I have borrowed your life and allowed myself to be struck by your courage, by Irina's gentleness, Igor's wisdom and the qualities of the other characters, who together are part of the choir of voices that forms the basis of an intense and overwhelming story.
  Some love stories are gifted with an extraordinary strength that needs to be told, and the love between yourself and Irina is one of these. With this in mind, I am writing to inform you that I would be delighted to accept your offer of allowing me to write a novel.
  I already have the title in mind: Come With Me. I will let you read it as soon as it is finished.
Kind regards
  Pier Giorgio Casali

Notes

1. These sentences summarise comments heard by the writer Ines Belski Lagazzi (1908–2003) during her extensive travels in the USSR/Russia.
2. 'They're coming. They're going to take me to Vladivostock. Come and get me.'
3. *Samizdat* – a Russian term literally meaning 'self-publishing'. A phenomenon which arose spontaneously in the Soviet Union between the end of the Fifties and the early Sixties and which consisted of the secret distribution of illegal publications which had been censored by the regime's authorities.
4. 'To your fragile and eternal beauty, I love you.'
5. The Autonomous National University of Mexico.

About the Author

Nicola Viceconti is a prize-winning Italian writer, poet and sociologist with a passion for the history and culture of Latin America with particular reference to the role of human rights. He has published ten works (novels, poems, and short stories) five of which were released simultaneously in Italy and Argentina, and also distributed in Cuba and Chile. The Chamber of Deputies of the Province of Buenos Aires bestowed upon him the prestigious title of *Visitante Ilustre* (Honoured Guest) for his work in keeping alive the history of the Argentinian people through his novels, which portray significant historical moments in contemporary culture and politics.